THE ROAD TO SOMEWHERE

THE·PIPER··

THE ROAD
TO SOMEWHERE

By
ENID DINNIS

It was so straight, it was so strange,
To right, to left, it did not range,
The Road that led to somewhere.

It was so strange, it was so straight,
It led one to a golden gate,
And Love took Wonder for his mate
And Life Went on to Somewhere.

ST. AIDAN PRESS, LLC
Morning View, Kentucky

The Road to Somewhere.

First published in 1927 by B. Herder Book Co., St. Louis, MO, and Sands & Co., London & Edinbugh. Reprinted using B. Herder edition.

Typesetting, layout and cover design copyright 2024 St. Aidan Press, LLC.

Cover art is the frontispiece of the B. Herder edition.

ISBN-13: 978-1-962503-06-8
ISBN-10: 1-962503-06-2

For more information, contact:
www.staidanpress.com
staidanpress@gmail.com

We have made no intentional change from the original text except to correct mistakes in spelling and punctuation.

CONTENTS

THE ROAD
TO SOMEWHERE

Prologue

T WAS QUITE a large company—large in the sense of numbers, that is—some of its members, little Ann Perivale, for instance, were quite small, which had gathered round the Wishing Well, following the instructions of the smooth-voiced Dictator who conducted the circular tour. The programme demanded that each member should formulate a wish over the magic waters—it was the light relief after the rather stodgy Roman remains—and everyone rose sportingly to the occasion, with the exception of Philip's uncle, Mr. Silas Bulkington, M.P., who had no truck with magic wells. (They had hardly begun to yield petrol in the year 1910.) He was eminently a person who would depend on the water-works.

The bevy of youngsters who formed part of the company entered into the proceedings with a zest that amused the grownups. All the grown-ups, that is, except Ann's mother who didn't approve of superstition. She had refused to explore a show church, on account of ritualistic notices exhibited outside, and had kept Ann with her when the others went in because the child was so impressionable. As for Ann, she was taking it all with profound seriousness. She stood there fairly vibrating with the intensity of the moment. Her eldest sister, Beryl, had just wished. The wishing, it seemed had to be done out loud, which was embarrassing. "Lots of money" had been Beryl's challenge to the presiding genius of the well. Doris, her other sister, came along next and wished, with the utmost frankness, that someone might want to marry her when she grew up. That was tiresome of Doris, because Philip, Ann's beloved playmate, whom she loved more than all her brothers and sisters put together, was standing there listening. His Uncle Silas had forbidden him to take part in the tomfoolery, and Philip himself didn't look as though he believed in it, but he would be dreadfully hurt if she didn't make the same request as Doris because Philip always said that he meant to marry her, and he might think that she didn't want to marry him. Moreover, he might think that the wish which was the wish of her heart was ever so silly.

It had come to Ann's turn. The little circle looking on was amused at the intense earnestness of the small, dark-eyed child with the original little face. She was pressing her arms close to her sides, her hands were clenched into two tight little fists. It all suggested the intense physical effort involved in "wishing with all one's might."

"I wish," Ann said, "I wish"—she flushed and stammered—"I wish that the—the once-upon-a-time things were true."

There was a little laugh. Ann blushed. Her voice had been made courageously audible. Then someone said:

"You would like things to happen once upon *this* time?"

Ann surveyed the speaker. It was the clergyman who had been making them all laugh on the journey with Irish stories. He was quite serious now, when everyone else was laughing. He seemed to understand what she meant. He was not like the clergymen she was used to.

"They never do," she said, with a shake of her head.

The other glanced at the little face with the big, soft eyes that suggested Latin blood. The mother was so very Anglo-Saxon.

He lingered by the well when the others had moved off, murmuring to himself, "poor little kiddie!"

"That was a holy well," he told his travelling companion, when he rejoined him, "I stayed behind to say a prayer to the saint-in-charge." A shock did Rolt good—he was a new convert.

"Really! I thought it was a sort of fairy business; but I believe you regard the fairies as angels in their week-day frocks. What did you wish—I mean pray for?"

"That that kiddie might get what she asked for," was the reply.

Chapter One

A LARGE AND DULY detailed map of London and its environs lay spread out on the dining-room table of No. 6 Taplow Square, London, W., but if you had wished to consult it you would have met with an obstacle in the shape of two heads placed close together. One was fair and curly, the other dark and smooth: the fair head belonged to Philip Hallidan, and the dark, bobbed one to Ann Perivale. I hope this is clear?

Egbert, the black cat, was the only other occupant of the room. He suffered engaged couples gladly, or at least without comment, and Philip and Ann were engaged to the point of house-hunting. Hence the consultation over the outspread map.

House-finding is an agreeable enough occupation when the question of money is not too pressing, and Philip and Ann were starting life under particularly pleasant circumstances. Philip's uncle, Mr. Silas Bulkington, of Bulkington and Bulkington, the big oil people, had taken the question of a house in hand. His nephew's means would not run to buying a house worth living in, and houses to let were few and far between. "Look out for a house to suit your fancy," Uncle Silas said, "and I will buy it, and then—we will see." Uncle Silas never did anything in a hurry, he acted with the caution maliciously attributed to the Scot, but his "we'll see" was quite a safe thing to go upon, so the young couple embarked upon their house-hunting under the ægis of Mr. Bulkington, the oil magnate, and his prodigious banking account.

The question of neighbourhoods had to be approached from the point of view of a young person of a romantic turn of mind. Somewhere where Dick Turpin used to rob and ride away, leaving behind him the odour of Romance, was Ann's desideratum—she was very young and only just growing out of Grimm's fairy tales. Philip gave due consideration to train services, being one of those who go up to the city in trains. He ran his finger over the green patches on the map and each suburb came in for its scrutiny. It was a difficult point to decide.

At length Egbert came to the rescue. He sprang from his seat on the back of the sofa and alighted with feline grace and exactitude on the edge of the map. He ran his eye over the green patches under consideration, focused it, and then stretching out a paw placed it gently but deliberately on the lower left-hand corner of the map, in the centre of Richstead Common.

"There! Egbert has settled it for us," Ann cried, delightedly. "He always does." She picked up the sleek animal and bestowed on it a well-earned hug. "It has got to be Richstead Common. We might have gone on all night trying to decide."

"The trains to Richstead are quite good," Philip admitted.

"And it has got lovely historical associations," Ann reminded him. "There used to be a castle there, and a palace, and a monastery." Her words rather trailed off. She had been told dreadful stories about the superstitious monks when she was a child. Her dead mother had found monks to be very terrible people. She was not sure that a monastery tradition fitted in.

"Well," Philip said, "Egbert has saved us tossing: heads, Dick Turpin; tails, the Abbot of Richstead. Long life to them both!"

"I'm not going to toast the Abbot of Richstead," Ann said, sturdily. "Those old monks were horribly wicked."

"Worse than Dick Turpin? Well, at any rate Snoburbia needs a counterpoise to its oppressive respectability. Here's to the ghost of the Abbot of Richstead. An innocuously transparent figure of romance."

Ann picked up Egbert. "Isn't he a silly creature?" she said to the cat. "You know, he won't be serious over anything that matters."

"Which means anything that never was nor could be," her *fiancé* interpolated, diverting Egbert's attention by pulling his whisker. "The sweet, impossible things that are essential to human happiness. Romance, fairy tales, 'Once-upon-a-time.'"

"If they were essential to human happiness they would not be impossible," Ann made the comment meditatively rather than dogmatically. Then she added: "It would be ripping if they were true."

"The Abbot? Dick Turpin?" But he had teazed her enough.

"Sweet, impossible thing!" Philip said. "Egbert is asking you to let him out of the door. *He* wants his dinner. Egbert has an inconsequent mind."

Philip and Ann stood at the end of the avenue where the 'bus from Charing Cross puts you down if the conductor doesn't forget. They were engaged in the delightful but slightly fatiguing task of inspecting likely residences in the select suburb of Richstead. Quite a goodly selection of Georgian villas bore the legend, "to be sold," and they had explored a fair number and were beginning to get a little back-achy when they came upon Richstead Avenue. Unlike most suburban avenues it fully justified its appellation. A line of tall elm trees of the immemorial order rose on either side and conducted the eye along a vista which appeared to be luring one away from the bricks and mortar of Richstead Broadway to a somewhere which the height and dignity of the elms suggested might be a place of importance. Behind the elms, well set back and peeping between them, were a series of rather superior residences of the villa type. They varied pleasingly both in size and appearance, the mood of the architect having changed, apparently, at each house.

Ann fell in love with the avenue on the spot. "I wonder where it leads to?" she cried; "what glorious trees! And don't the houses look exactly as though they were peeping through at something? I wonder where it leads to?"

Philip, ever practical as Ann was ever imaginative, turned round and detained a boy with a grocer's basket on his arm. "Here, Tommy," he cried, "where does that lead to?"

The grocer's messenger glanced up the avenue. "It don't lead to nowhere," he replied, laconically.

Now Philip happened to possess the regrettable habit of catching people up. A horrid habit, although Philip was not in the least a horrid person. "Then it leads to somewhere," he affirmed, inviting altercation.

The grocer's boy hadn't a notion what he was driving at. For him, being no grammarian, a double negative gave due and legitimate emphasis to a statement. "It don't lead to nowhere," he repeated, patiently.

"Oh! Doesn't that sound delicious!" Ann broke in. "A road to Nowhere. Do let's come and see what is at the other end." She rewarded their informant with a smile that made amends for her *fiancé's* pedantry and turned Philip gently in the desired direction.

They walked up the avenue, glancing at the houses on either side. "We'll come back and look at the houses," Ann said. "First do let us find out where this leads to."

"It leads to nowhere," her *fiancé* reminded her. "We shall find a stile leading to the Never-never Land. That would just suit you, Nankin."

The sheltering elms conducted them onward. "Doesn't it feel as though some old-world procession had passed along here?" Ann said, "and as if the houses were spectators watching the ghost of the procession pass."

"Exactly," Philip said, dangerously, "look at that one peeping at us with both its best bedroom windows. It is winking its left window-blind, I do believe."

Ann kept up the rally. "That's because it knows that we are out on the road to Nowhere, like the ghosts." She was not sure that she was quite pleased with her rejoinder.

"I believe there is something passing along now!" Philip shuddered magnificently. "Look at that house with the pointed gables pricking its ears. It's exactly like a fox terrier when someone says, 'rats.'"

"Rats!" Ann retorted. "It has heard that a certain boy and girl are passing this way." She broke off. "But what a strange place it is—the house that is pricking its gable. Why, it is an *old* house! As old as the hills! Philip, we must be dreaming!"

Chapter Two

HERE WAS NO mistaking that Ann was right. Two Gables rose from the centre of a newly laid-out plot of land in startling incongruity to its surroundings. The decrepitude of age was suggested by the overhanging eaves, with their warped timbers. The red tiled roof, the twisted chimney stacks, all pointed to the fact that an ancient English dwelling-house had sprung into being in Richstead Avenue. There it stood, huddled to itself, as though conscious of its uncongenial surroundings; aloof from its new-rich neighbours, and shuddering under the cold stare of the Victorian Tower House opposite.

Well might they think they were dreaming!

"Look! It's to be sold!"

Ann cried out with such a degree of ecstasy in her voice that it summoned the custodian of the spectral domicile to their side. He came forward from where he was at work in the grounds and invited inspection, as he might have done for any post-War jerry-built villa. Yes, Two Gables was for sale. A unique chance for anyone with a taste for antiquities. The house had been practically brought from the country and re-built here. The timbers, tiles, fittings, everything except the bare walls, had been part of Digley Grange in Xshire. There had been a fuss about the demolishing of the old place, the intelligent custodian told them. There were stories of hidden treasure, and other legends connected with it. Ann drew him out whilst Philip made enquiries about the bathroom. It was becoming more and more thrilling and ghostified, and everything that was desirable.

Philip, having settled the question of a geyser, went on to enquire: "How about the family ghost? I presume it has been transferred with the other fittings?"

"There would be quite enough atmosphere to support a ghost," Ann declared. She was gazing through the leaded panes of the long, low window in the panelled dining-room. My Lady in her Elizabethan ruff would have gazed through those very same panes. "Phil, we must have Two Gables. Do you think Uncle Silas would rise to it?"

"He might, if the hidden treasure were tucked away in one of the transmitted parts," her *fiancé* said. The caretaker had gone off and left them to themselves—"Uncle Silas likes to do a little deal with a sound investment. But in any case one could easily sell this place for double they are asking for it. The owner hasn't realized its value."

"Oh, look at the latch-strings!" Ann was fingering the leather string which took the place of a handle on the door. "And the same on the scullery door as the drawing-room. What a joy! You will never be able to call it 'Snoburbia' again."

"Well, that settles it," Philip said.

To the left of the porch a quaintly carved wooden head was speeding the parting guest with tears—a smiling countenance, also carved in wood, had welcomed them from the right side. Ann was enchanted with the quaint device. "Two Gables is heavenly!" said she.

"We'll have a rockery and crazy paving," Philip said. He was an enthusiastic gardener. "What a jolly, little, curly path it is leading to the gate."

They passed through the little wooden gate and walked along, preoccupied by the matter in hand. October was not a bad month to get married in. They were not going to wait for the spring, not they!

A slight autumnal mist was gathering as they reached the end of the avenue. "Let's see," Philip said, "the agent's place was at the corner on the left, wasn't it?"

The road had terminated suddenly, as roads do on which two people deeply interested in each other walk and talk. They had already veered to the left when they uttered a simultaneous exclamation. In front of them was no high road. On the left, no estate office! Before them lay a stretch of country veiled in the gathering mist. For just a moment they were silent. Then they both burst out laughing.

"We've come the wrong way," Ann said. "Of course, how stupid! We crossed the road to look at Two Gables, and forgot. But what a delicious mistake. I thought we really had come upon the Never-never Land."

"I confess I did feel creepy up my back," Philip admitted. "I completely forgot that we had crossed the road. I suppose this must be Richstead Common. We will explore it one day. The Never-never Land may lie out beyond."

They stood for a moment gazing out into the misty distance. It was an uncultivated stretch of heathland, wooded and undulating.

"We shall be able to wander out into the country," Philip said. "The road did lead to somewhere, after all."

They turned round, half reluctantly. But the practical business of the estate agent would not wait. Two Gables gave them a fresh shock as they came upon it. It looked older and more romantic than ever, and more aloof and misplaced in its juxtaposition to the garish Broadlands and its fellow-villas.

The name of Uncle Silas was one to conjure with at an estate agent's office. Not many minutes later Philip and Ann were back on the Broadway waiting for the 'bus to take them back to town.

As they stood waiting for the vehicle of the common herd Ann looked about her. Perambulators were being pushed to and fro by nursemaids or mothers, as the case might be, who gazed wistfully into the windows of the smart array of shops, in search of something new and alluring.

"I hope you won't get fed up with this sort of thing, Nan," Philip said, rather anxiously. "Of course, we shall have the car, and you can get away as much as you like."

But Ann was out to be pleased with everything. The Broadway was not the faerie end of the avenue, she admitted, but it was far from hopeless. "Look!" she cried, "at that old man playing a whistle. Doesn't he look exactly as though he had borrowed his pipe from Pan?"

The old man in question was standing on the curb, a not unpicturesque study in black and white. His clothes were rusty black, and his thick hair and beard snowy white. He was engaged in piping out a cheerful ditty on an instrument of the flute order, plainly a home-made one. It had a singularly sweet tone. Philip was tickled at Ann's remark. Pan piping for the mild orgy of suburban shop-gazing. Such a very aged, shabby, and infirm Pan it was, too.

Suddenly, as they watched him, Pan changed his tune. He started to pipe an outrageously merry stave. A kind of jig that contained magic in its measure. Ann's feet refused to keep still as she listened. "Why, Phillikin! He's the pied piper of Hamelin," she cried. "Wouldn't it be topping if he set all the people here dancing and led them away to the Never-never Land?"

She was delighted with the idea. "Can't you see all the perambulators following, and the respectable housewives—like I'm going to be—and the Vicar on his way to pay parochial calls, and the butcher boy with the beef for next door? What a priceless old person he is!"

Her feet were disporting themselves suspiciously, even as

she spoke. "There! Isn't my idea much prettier than yours, you old cynic?"

"It's gorgeous," her *fiancé* agreed. "Let's give the old boy a bob."

He made it half-a-crown, and the pied piper was delighted with his honorarium. He touched his hat, then pointed to a slate which hung in front of him. On it was written: "Dumb." He then pointed to his pipe, smiled—an extraordinarily sweet smile, as engaging as the melody he had been playing—and shook his head with emphasis.

It was Philip who tumbled to his meaning first. "The pipe speaks all right," he said. "It speaks for you, eh?"

The old man nodded, delighted. He tapped the half-crown with his finger. Then, having removed his cap and tucked it under his arm, played the opening bars of "God save the King"; after which with a bow he prepared to move off. The windfall had enabled him to close down for the day.

"What a perfectly enchanting old person!" Ann said. She watched him as he walked away. "I believe if he were to play a tune as he went along everyone would have to follow him."

The manager of the Pure Bread Bakeries happened to be standing at his door. He overheard the remark and smiled blandly. A carefully cultivated instinct told him that the young couple might be potential customers: he hastened to cast his bread upon the waters, as became one of his calling.

"One of our Richstead characters," he observed, urbanely. "The old gentleman is a very well-known personage about here. He lives up on the common, and as often as not he plays a tune as he walks home. Quite a character, he is."

He receded into his shop, with a smile and a bow, to attend to a customer.

Ann was triumphant. "There," she cried. "He *is* a pied piper! What an utterly delicious place this is. I do hope he walks home up our avenue. I am perfectly convinced it must have led to somewhere in the old days, and I'm sure the old piper could tell us if only he could speak."

"He can pipe," Philip reminded her. He put a tone of due concern into his voice. Their 'bus had drawn up, and he bundled her into it. "There," he observed, with a sigh of relief, "I'm downright thankful that I've got you in safely. I should have had to call a taxi if this hadn't come along. The old man might have started his tune any minute."

Ann received her due amount of chaff from the family circle over her description of the faerie grange, exiled into villadom and breathing the atmosphere of Marianna. The younger members were thrilled by the legend of the hidden treasure. It was universally hoped that Uncle Silas would rise to the purchase of Two Gables.

As for Mr. Bulkington, he absorbed Philip's statement as to the bargain presented by the genuine old Tudor house which its present owner was offering for sale at the price of a modern one. Then he arranged for the young couple to pilot him in his car to Richstead Avenue, so that he might inspect Two Gables personally.

His approval was a foregone conclusion. Ann, if not Philip, could generally do what she liked with Uncle Silas.

Two Gables welcomed them with what Philip called the "wipe in the eye" that its incongruous antiquity gave the new-comer.

Uncle Silas was impressed. He followed his nephew through the panelled rooms and up the carved oak staircase with growing approbation. He became informative and enlarged upon the spacious days of good Queen Bess. Queen Bess was included by him among the seven heroines of Christendom. Uncle Silas knew some history. He used it on the political platform at election time. Very queer history it was, but you don't expect much at an election. He waxed facetious over the story of the hidden treasure. It was an oversight that it hadn't been brought along with the other characteristic bits.

"And the family ghost would have come out and shown us where to look for it," Ann said. "I wonder if the ghost has come along?" Philip shook his head, sadly. "All the family ghosts have been bought up by the spiritists," he sighed. "So are the mighty fallen."

Mr. Bulkington relapsed into the matter of fact. He disliked superstition connected with religion. Not that spiritism savoured of Romanism, but it was tainted with the supernatural, a dangerous thing in any religion. "We must get to business," he said. So they got to business.

Uncle Silas made matters perfectly clear. Before making the young couple a present of the house he wished to have his say as to the adjustment of certain details. The leather latchstrings did not please him, for one thing, and there were stipulations as to certain things, and suggestions which had to be fallen in with before Two Gables became Uncle Silas's wedding gift to his nephew.

The garden next claimed their attention. Philip was aching to get to work on it. He proposed taking up his residence at once and occupying the early daylight hours before going to business in getting it into order, but Mr. Bulkington remembered that this would involve the payment of rates and taxes on an inhabited house.

Then it was that Philip hit on the ingenious idea of acting as caretaker. He had roughed it in his time and could very easily get his own breakfast in the morning.

"What a splendid idea!" Ann cried. "And you may meet the family ghost, all by yourself in the empty house. It sounds quite too deliciously creepy."

So the arrangement was made that Philip should take over the caretaker's job. A small room at the back was already furnished for the purpose, and Philip, as he said, had roughed it. The electric light and gas were both laid on, and he could light up his fire if he felt chilly. The telephone, moreover, was ready at hand. He and Ann stood together after Uncle Silas had shot off in his car—Uncle Silas was always on the move—and took stock once more of their surroundings. Two Gables would require some keeping up, but Uncle Silas was in a generous mood; and there was that appointment waiting for Philip in the Firm when a certain person's time came to retire. Golden prospects opened out before the happy pair, who passed out together through the wooden gate at the end of the curly path. Ann glanced up the avenue. Its air of well-being was typical of what Philip had called "Snoburbia." "It *doesn't* lead to nowhere," she affirmed with defiant conviction.

"We will go and see directly we get a chance," Philip said.

Chapter Three

THE PURCHASE of Two Gables had been negotiated, and Philip Hallidan duly installed in the office of caretaker. He occupied the only furnished room in the house, in which to the ordinary atmosphere of an empty house was added the creepiness which had delighted Ann's heart.

Carpenters and decorators were in possession in the day-time, making some structural alterations suggested by Mr. Bulkington; at night-time Philip shared it with the ghosts, who had not, so far, made their appearance. Every morning the early worm was incommoded by the spade or other implement of the ardent caretaker. Philip was getting the garden into something like shape; and at dusk the early ghost found him at the same task. The fact that the ghosts had not made their appearance did not necessarily mean that they were not there.

On Saturday Philip would be spending his holiday in the garden, and it was arranged that Ann should join him and lend a hand, and confer on the outstanding question of furnishing. Uncle Silas had made it clear that they might look to him in that matter, too.

Two Gables looked more aloof than ever as Ann walked up the avenue. Rather like a discomfited aristocrat in a middle-class assembly. The Tower House looked horribly blatant and self-satisfied. Its storied windows took no cognizance of the procession that passed between the elms, only, it might be, of the delinquencies of its opposite neighbours. Ann took a cordial dislike to the Tower House.

She found Philip busy in the back garden, and they worked solidly for an hour. Then the idea of lunch suggested itself, and a quiet confab as to the correct style of furniture for a Tudor house. They had seen a Sale by Auction advertised where antique pieces of furniture, oak chests, warming-pans, grandfather's clocks, and such like would be procurable. Two Gables had got to be furnished in character with its ancient beams and latch-strings. Philip was to get Monday off from his office and they were going to set about it all.

Ann had very definite ideas on the matter. She and Philip settled themselves down to lunch magnificently, the deep window seat in the dining-room serving as a table for their repast, and a, or rather, *the* chair from the caretaker's room and the floor, for sitting accommodation.

Philip sat hugging his knees. He had finished his third jam tart, following on a goodly number of assorted sandwiches out of Ann's magic bag—she had insisted on bringing lunch. Suddenly he asked her a question, right off the point they were discussing. He spoke with some hesitation:

"What effect has Two Gables on you, Nan? I hope you won't get hipped here by yourself."

"You silly boy," she said. "There is an eerie feeling, I admit, but I love it. I hope *you* aren't getting hipped, alone at night in an empty house with the ghost. I wonder if it hunts for the missing treasure?"

They sat in silence listening to the sound made by the carpenter who was still at work sawing wood. It was nearly time for him to stop.

Ann was gazing through the long, low window with its diamond panes, the old original glass of Digley Manor.

"Do you think the Tower House would allow us to have the pied piper to supper?" she queried. "He recognized me and smiled this morning, and gave me a little tune all to myself." She was surveying their *vis-à-vis* defiantly through the Elizabethan glass.

"We should have to send the servants out. Ann, you're a revolutionary."

"Wouldn't it be strange," she went on, "if one were to see only people in doublets and hooped skirts and ruffs when one looked out through ancient casements? Imagine a man in a big cloak and a curly hat coming up the path instead of Uncle Silas, or Tom in his plus fours."

"Take care," Philip said, "that has a smack of Guy Fawkes about it. He was worse than Dick Turpin. Those heroes of the past are best left to their own generation."

Ann knew that he was laughing at her. "I believe all the old glass does is to make the Tower House look even more horridly new and banal," she said. "I don't like the Tower House. It suggests the road to Nowhere, in a nasty limited sort of sense—Nowhere in particular, I mean."

"Going round and round instead of on ahead?" Philip had quite a neat way of putting things sometimes.

The sound of sawing had ceased and stillness, grateful to the ear, reigned in its stead. Ann lapsed into silence. Richstead Common Avenue was made up of Tower Houses. She was glad to feel that the open country lay beyond—that they had obtained a glimpse of Fairyland for the tenth part of a second when they stood on its edge. That had been a salutary peep!

Her lover sat watching her. Ann's face when she was in a reverie was a pleasant thing to watch, even if you were not her lover. "Oh, dear," he said, "I wish I could buy the moon. I believe it's exactly the wedding present you would have liked if you had had the choice. Two Gables is second best."

There came a tap on the door, interrupting Ann's disclaimer. The carpenter who had been making the noise stood without. He had a consequential air about him.

"If you and the lady would just step round," the carpenter said to Philip, "I'd like to show you something queer about the beam as I have just been sawing through, before I go off."

He led the way, across the hall to the place where he had been at work. A long oaken beam lay there sawn through the centre. Their guide struck it with his fist. "It's 'oller, that beam," he said. "There's a longish hole in the middle of it. What they calls an haperture." The superfluous aspirate gave due dignity to the sufficiently arresting announcement.

He proceeded to show them the cavity. It was, plainly, a place of concealment cunningly contrived in the beam. For a moment both Philip and Ann were reduced to speechlessness. Then Ann cried: "It must be the place where they hid the treasure!" She was half joking, half in earnest.

"There ain't nothing in it," the workman said. "Not as far as I can tell. I put my arm right the way along; then I came and told you," he added, virtuously. He had an honest face and certainly didn't look as though he had treasure trove concealed about him.

"We'll try and find out," Philip said. "I've got an unusually long arm."

He bent down and thrust his arm into the hollow space. Ann stood by, breathless. It was bewilderingly story-booky.

"By Jove! There is something! Phew!"

Philip was struggling to add an inch to the natural length of his arm, and it was a rather painful effort. His finger tips had encountered something. He could just touch but not grip the thing which was there. He withdrew his arm and rubbed it, making a wry face. "That was rather a tax on the muscles," he observed, wincing. "Rather like the rack. I must get a stick."

Ann had flown to fetch the necessary implement. She returned, and the crooked handle of a walking stick effected what was required.

"It's heavy," Philip said. "It feels like a box of money." He thrust back his maltreated arm and extracted the object which had lain hidden at the far end of the cavity.

It was an oblong slab of stone to which were still clinging a few fragments of a perished silk covering.

"What on earth is it?" Philip said. He examined it curiously. The stone was about a foot in length and perhaps half an inch in thickness. There were five marks engraved on it. One at each corner and one in the centre.

"Whatever can it be?" Ann echoed. "What do those little crosses mean?"

"Must have been there hundreds of years," the carpenter observed, contributing a picturesque if obvious suggestion. "Looks like one of the stones they've got ready for the paving in the garden. Rum thing to be storing away a thing like that." With which comment he moved off, his half-day off having officially started.

Philip turned the stone over. "Wait a bit," he said, "there's something written on the back."

Words there certainly were, cut into the stone. It was quite easy to decipher them:

"Return me to James Laydon Prest."

Ann gazed at it, entranced. "I wonder what it means?" she said. "I wonder who James Laydon Prest was?"

"Well," Philip said. "Here's romance for you with a vengeance. Two Gables has risen gloriously to the occasion."

Ann regarded the cryptic signs on the stone. "It makes me feel funny all over," she declared, "but it is exciting. Much more exciting than a bag of ducats would have been. James Prest brings a real living personality into the story. I wonder if we shall see his ghost? We shall have to find out if the old family at Digley was called Prest."

"We'll ask Uncle Silas about it," Philip said. "He knows a lot about Elizabethan times, because of the Reformation."

"It's altogether heavenly," Ann said. "Can't you see Mr., or it may have been Sir James, Prest spreading his cloak under Queen Elizabeth's feet? Two Gables is a darling place to come up to the scratch like this. And it's real—frightfully real—not like the old antiques we are going to import from the Sale."

The afternoon brought Mr. Bulkington in his car to cast an eye over the alterations. It was characteristic of Uncle Silas that he kept an eye on the property which was still his. He was realizing more and more what a fine deal could have been done with the house which he was presenting to his nephew. He was to spend the week-end electioneering on an anti-ritualistic platform. Mr. Bulkington had a "down" on the Revised Prayer Book, and everybody else seemed to have an "up," if modern parlance contains such an expression. It was in a somewhat captious mood that Uncle Silas arrived.

Ann was bubbling over with the news of the discovery. The story of the hidden treasure had been a joke into which even Uncle Silas had entered, so far as he could enter into such a side issue as a joke. Mr. Bulkington was taken at once to the spot where the discovery had been made. First they showed him the hollow beam, then the mysterious stone, which had been placed on the old oaken mantel-piece over the open grate in the hall.

"What do you make of it, Uncle?" Philip asked.

Mr. Bulkington's behaviour from the moment that he started scrutinizing the stone became quite out of the ordinary. Philip and Ann watched him in wonder. What had happened to Uncle Silas? His behaviour was most peculiar. First he peered closely at the stone. Then he pursed up his lips. His eye gleamed. Instinctively he receded to a little distance from the object under scrutiny.

Then Uncle Silas spoke.

"Do you know what that is?" he said. "That's an altar stone. My stars and garters! The rogues! The cunning foxes!"

Chapter Four

UNCLE SILAS stood there wrought to a kind of fine frenzy. "The rogues! The cunning foxes!" he repeated.

Philip waited, giving a loose rein to Uncle Silas in a rhetorical mood, then he observed:

"It seems to have belonged to someone of the name of Prest—James Laydon Prest." He picked up the stone and showed the back to the other.

"Prest?" Uncle Silas echoed. "*Priest!* That's what you mean." He glared at the inscription on the back of the stone which his nephew was holding, refraining himself from undue contact with it. "They couldn't even spell properly, the rascals! They hid them away like that along with the rest of their trumpery— those popish priests that Walsingham set dancing on the end of a rope when they tried to say their Mass in Free England. Cunning dogs! They got short shrift when they were caught. They used to carry these stones about with them and make altars of them to say their Mass on. Even the rack couldn't stop 'em doing it, the bloodthirsty knaves!"

Uncle Silas paused. Ann had been duly impressed. She gave a shudder. A sinister vision of a black-coated Guy Fawkes figure, wearing a curly hat rose in her mind.

"How horrible!" she said. "And I had been thinking that Two Gables had such a nice atmosphere."

Philip's comment came more slowly.

"They must have had some pluck," he said.

"Pluck? The devil's own pluck," Uncle Silas retorted. "But Walsingham was equal to them. You may be sure that stone there cost James Laydon his life."

Philip regarded the stone, which he had replaced on the ledge. "Poor beggar!" he ejaculated.

Uncle Silas eyed him sharply.

"What did you say?" he asked.

"I said, '*Poor* beggar.'"

It occurred to Ann that a lighter note might be seasonably introduced. Philip was evidently getting into one of his contrary moods. "The carpenter commented on its likeness to the stones we are putting down on the path," she observed. "He had a very practical mind."

Mr. Bulkington, to her surprise, received the unconsidered remark as an inspiration. "Why, the very thing," he cried. "Excellent! Just what our glorious reformers did with the altars in the churches. Stuck them down where the people had to tread on them. That was how popery was 'stamped out' in England." He glanced round at his audience. Philip had apparently missed the witticism about stamping out. He was looking decidedly glum.

"We'll take the good fellow's hint and find a use for this," Mr. Bulkington went on. "We'll let it into the garden path, and it can preach the glorious Reformation, which they are trying to undo as hard as they can, when the parson comes along to call on you, eh?"

He glanced at Philip. The latter was looking even more glum.

"You agree with me," Uncle Silas suggested. There was danger in his tone.

"I'm afraid I don't." There was even more danger in the tone of the response. "It seems to me a very cheap way of expressing one's convictions—especially compared with the way these poor fellows seem to have expressed theirs."

Mr. Bulkington glared in amazed disapproval at his nephew. "Explain yourself," he said. "I don't follow you."

"I mean," Philip said, rather awkwardly, "that it's not good enough. If one had suffered a bit for one's own convictions, it might be different; but even then, I don't see the force of desecrating something that another man held sacred." He reddened.

Mr. Bulkington reddened likewise. Ann went a trifle pale. Uncle Silas was taking a long time to make his reply. What had possessed Philip?

"Well," Uncle Silas said, at length, "this is my house and I will see that it *is* done. If you don't approve you can go and live elsewhere. I warned you," he went on, coolly, "that there would be a few conditions if I made the place over to you."

Ann came to the rescue. Philip was in one of his obstinate moods—she had known him to stick like that over the question of having an *e* in the middle of the word 'judgement.' "That settles it," she said, in the lightest tones at her command. "You need not worry, Phil, if you have that feeling about it. Uncle Silas is taking all the responsibility. He and I are iconoclasts," she added, and laughed rather constrainedly.

Philip answered: "I'm not much of a religionist," he said, addressing his uncle. "I suppose I'm a pagan, though I go to church to please Nan, but I'm not a cad, I hope." He reddened again and looked away from his uncle's searching eye. He had hit out rather harder than he meant to.

Mr. Bulkington eyed him narrowly. He mistrusted the way in which his nephew failed to meet his eye. He summed up the situation. "The trouble with you," he said, "is that you have got yourself mixed up with these Romanists—Papists or Anglican—whatever they like to call themselves."

Philip smiled. "I can swear to you, Uncle," he said, "that I am not a papist."

But Uncle Silas was no fool. "Not yet, perhaps," he said, "but you are trending that way. It is all for the best," he added, eyeing his nephew with due severity, "that Providence has put this practical means of proving you in my way. The throne of this country has been safeguarded for centuries by the coronation oath, as perhaps you are aware? I am willing to take this, this gesture, as a similar guarantee. You can think the matter over. If I find the stone in its place on the path the next time I come I shall know that I am not encouraging a Papist; in the embryo or otherwise."

Having delivered this speech, Mr. Bulkington turned and walked towards the dining-room. Popery had been switched off for the time being. He proceeded to inspect the various alterations in his usual crisp and businesslike way. He paused before the latch on the drawing-room door. "You are rather attached to that, aren't you?" he said to Ann. "Well, we'll let it be. It is in keeping with the rest, I suppose."

Ann welcomed the indication of returning good temper, with intense relief. After all, Uncle Silas had only been annoyed for the moment. She was more disturbed by what Philip had said when he called himself a pagan, and said that he only went to church to please her. That was terribly wicked of Philip. Church-going was a grim duty in the school of morality in which Ann had been brought up. It yielded none of the delights which she had somehow never ceased to look for, but it was wrong of Philip to pretend that he was a pagan.

When Uncle Silas prepared to take his leave it would have appeared that the trouble had completely blown over. He nodded farewell to Philip as he stood on the door-step. Then he walked a little way down the path and paused. Philip and Ann had both been at work on the crazy paving. Already some of it was completed. Mr. Bulkington stood still. He pointed with his walking stick. "That's about the size," he said, "you can put the stone there." He dug at the existing stone with his stick, then stooping down dislodged it and threw it on one side. Uncle Silas was nothing if not practical.

He took a sharp glance at his nephew's face. "As soon as you have got it into place you can start choosing your furniture," Mr. Bulkington said. "I shouldn't recommend you to do so before." He had fired his shot most effectively.

Philip and Ann watched the retreating figure of Uncle Silas. They watched his car drive off. Then Ann felt it was time to say something. But the right something was difficult to find.

At that moment the silence was invaded by a strange sound. It was a tune played in the distance on a soft, flute-like instrument.

"I believe it's the old piper," Ann cried, thankful for the interruption. "He is playing 'Land of hope and glory,' only he has improved on it. He might have enchanted Uncle Silas if he had been walking."

"I am afraid Uncle Silas is not a very enchantable subject." Philip said it grimly. "He always walks to a tune of his own making, and he wouldn't be likely to keep step with a pied piper."

"I do hope he won't be tiresome about the—the stone," Ann said. "At least," she added, coming to the point, "I hope *you* won't be tiresome, Phil. You know Uncle Silas has to be humoured. He has been awfully good about the furniture—I've got him round to agree that the original old oak won't be too extravagant."

Philip thrust out his underlip. He said nothing. It was not promising. "You know you can't help yourself in the circumstance," Ann ventured to add.

Her *fiancé* thrust his hands into his pockets. He walked over to the window and stared out at the Tower House.

"Can't I?" he queried. "I suppose I can't. I suppose I am the creature of Uncle Silas."

"But, Phil, I gave in about the door latch, and see how nice he was in the end."

He turned round. This was an entirely new Philip.

"So you take this as being on a level with the question of the door-handle?"

Ann became suddenly frightened. "Phil. Don't be an obstinate old goose. It isn't as though you were in sympathy with these awful Romanists. Uncle Silas is quite right to be down on them."

"Suppose we turn to the non-controversial question of the rockery?"

Philip was certainly not himself. "We must settle definitely where it is to be before Tom turns up to fetch you."

Ann's brother Tom had promised to fetch her home in his side-car. He was a somewhat erratic youth and not to be counted upon to turn up. They worked for an hour in the garden without any sign of him. Then Ann decided that she would go home by 'bus. It had been a shadowed hour. They had joked about the rockery, but the little differences of opinion had lost their savour. Philip fell in with all her suggestions and overlooked her ignorances with unwonted docility. Was it that some baleful influence had crept over Two Gables? Neither of them spoke any more of James Laydon, to whose name was attached the sinister affix of "prest." The stone lay, stark and unsightly, on the mantelpiece, a grim piece of realism, when they attempted to discuss the contemporary oak chest that was to be obtained by hook or by crook for the dining-room. No more allusion was made to the family ghost. Yet it had been such a dramatic and story-booky discovery.

They left the house together in the gathering gloom of the late October afternoon. Ann glanced up the road towards the common. She longed to engage Philip in the controversy as to whether it led to Somewhere, or Nowhere, but the "shadow" prevented that. They were horribly matter-of-fact at the present juncture.

On the Broadway Philip stood with her, waiting to put her on her 'bus. Tom had played them false. The old piper was standing at his pitch. He caught sight of them and greeted them with a change of tune. The merry note of greeting selected was not perhaps the most appropriate to their mood, though, possibly, on the other hand, it might have served to modify it, the piper being of the faerie kind, only at that moment their attention was diverted by a cheerful "Hullo!"

It was Tom. "Sorry I was late," he said as he dismounted from his bike. Tom always took things easily. "Lucky I twigged you. Well, how goes everything? Any news of the hidden treasure?"

It was exactly the question Tom would have elected to ask. Philip waited for Ann to answer, and Ann waited for Philip. The pied piper had ceased piping, realizing perhaps that he might be distracting. He gave the impression of having the manners of a gentleman.

Philip took the situation in hand. He proceeded to relate the afternoon's discovery, avoiding Uncle Silas's contribution to the story.

"Some treasure!" Tom laughed. "An old stone with scratches on it! But it's rather interesting—the name I mean. Did anybody named—what did you say? Laydon—ever live at Two Gables when it disported itself at what's the name of the place in the country?"

"I might be able to find out," Philip said. He opened the door of the side-car.

"Hop in, old girl," Tom said. "Bye-bye, Phil. Be good! and don't have words with the ghost. If it's a cheerful kind it may keep you company. Engagement in town? That's better. You'll be getting jim-jams in that empty place."

Chapter Four

Ann hopped in obediently. She caught sight of the old piper. What a beautiful old face he had. He was not piping now. Someone, a soldier in the kilt of a highland regiment, came along and threw a coin into his hat that stood beside him on the pavement. It recalled him to business. He placed the flute to his lips and served out the money's worth. As they started off, intermingled with the noise of Tom's engine, came the tender strains of "Will ye no come back again?"

Chapter Five

THE ENGAGEMENT in town served to keep Philip away from his ghosts until quite late in the evening. He returned to his lonely haunt somewhere near the witching hour to ruminate over the situation. He had no inclination to go to bed. He felt too wretched. Nan was vexed with him. A shadow had fallen between them. Uncle Silas's attitude was negligible compared with that. Nan had failed to see his point, that was the ghastly thing. She thought it was just cussedness on his part. Perhaps it was? Perhaps he had been a fool? It was one thing to refuse to play the cad to please Uncle Silas and another to do a thing in order to save the feelings of Nan. After all, he had a duty to her which took the caddishness out of the action.

He was tired of pacing about his room, the little back room which had been furnished for the caretaker. He walked out into the hall, switched on the light, and had another look at the stone which had caused all the trouble. Uncle Silas had made it clear—their first piece of "antique furniture" had got to be put into its place before they started turning over Crampton's stock. He had arranged to take that day off from the office so that he and Ann might go to Crampton's, and on to the auction where the mistletoe-bough chest was likely to be going at a reasonable price. Uncle Silas had been very generous about the furnishing. He was going to be out of town for the next day or two, speaking at an election, so his next visit to Two Gables was not imminent. But—the stone had got to be in its position before he came. Uncle Silas had advised prudence in the matter of the furnishing arrangements. The placing of the stone had got to come first.

Philip returned to his room. It was a comfortless hole, but it was not so beastly as the rest of the place. The empty house with its hollow sounds and creaks, was apt to get a bit on one's nerves. He settled down in the arm-chair—the one he had wheeled into the dining-room for Ann to have her lunch in style. That wretched discovery had seemed to change the whole atmosphere of the place. They had been so jolly at lunch. Yes, he had certainly played the fool with Uncle Silas.

Why the dickens hadn't he brought in something to read? Philip felt the creepiness of the place getting into his spine. He remembered that there might be an *Evening News* in his overcoat pocket. He went over and searched. But the overcoat pocket, alack! yielded no *Evening News*. Perhaps it had fallen out in the hall as he came in? He went out again and switched on the light in forlorn hope. He must have something to read. He peered round about him. There was no sign of anything lying on the floor. Yes, there was! In the corner, to the right of the front door, just under the telephone lay a small object. It was not a folded newspaper, but better still, it was a book! Philip stooped and picked up a small brown volume. It was old and much worn and bound in calf. It had certainly not been there before. They would not have failed to notice it when they took measurements for the rugs. Where on earth could it have sprung from?

Philip turned with some curiosity to the title-page. He read there an elaborate title: "Memoirs of Missionary Priests. As well secular as regular, and of other Catholics of both sexes, that have suffered death in England on religious accounts from the year of our Lord 1577 to 1634, gathered partly from printed accounts of their lives and sufferings, published by contemporary authors in diverse languages, and partly from manuscript relations, kept in the archives and records of the English colleges and convents and oftentimes penned by eyewitnesses of their death." The name of the compiler was then given: Richard Challoner, D.D.

There was a strip of paper marking a page in the middle of the book. Philip opened it at the place indicated and read:

"James Laydon, Priest. Hanged, drawn, and quartered at Tyburn, May 16th, 1595."

What was the meaning of it? Philip drew in a breath of wonder and bewilderment. Could it have dropped out of the hiding place as well as the stone? But that was impossible. They were all alert for findings, and it was nowhere near where the beam had been. The carpenter could hardly be implicated. There could be no motive for such conduct; and, the outstanding fact remained, the book had not been there all the time.

He gave up guessing and returned once more to his room. There he set a match to the fire and prepared to settle down and examine the contents of the book which had dropped from nowhere.

Here was some kind of clue. On the fly-leaf was written in faint ink a name: Cecil Carlyon, January, 1873. That would not necessarily be the name of its last owner. It was the kind of book that could be picked up second-hand. It appeared to contain memoirs of any number of Missionary Priests. There must have been scores of them! An idea struck him. Could Uncle Silas be responsible for the trick? He possessed a key to the house. What gruesome revelation of the iniquities of James Laydon would he find in the pages before him? He had been longing for a detective story to pass the time. He was in for something far more thrilling if this last surmise was right. Uncle Silas was not given to playing tricks, but one never knows.

The story of James Laydon was by no means lacking in the high colour that one connects with a "shocker," for all that it was told with an engaging simplicity. It possessed a vividness of style that fully atoned for the excessive amount of piety that was mingled with its other elements. Philip had not read many lines before he realized that Uncle Silas was absolved from the accusation of having had a hand in the placing of James Laydon's life in his nephew's hands.

James, who was born of parents who had conformed to the new religion under pressure of fines and imprisonment, besides being possessed of the Christian virtues had a lean, freckled face and also, his biographer was at pains to add, freckles on his hands. His eyes were greenish and he had red hair, and some hesitation in his speech. James had been dissatisfied with the religion that he found at Oxford and had ridden away one day with three companions and shipped for France, where they entered a college and got themselves ordained priests. Here James Laydon had hastened through his studies at a great pace, being anxious to return to England in time to reconcile his aged nurse to the true Church. Having accomplished this, he had traversed the country administering the sacraments and winning souls to God as much by his modest cheerfulness as by his holy life. James's modest "cheerfulness" seemed to embrace an incurable habit of cracking jokes and seeing the light side of things. He was finally captured by the Queen's pursuivants in the woods near Digley Grange, where he had been in the habit of saying Mass. They carried him to London loaded with chains, which were by no means removed when he was stricken with fever on the journey. A young Oxford student of arts who, moved with pity, endeavoured to give him some solace was himself apprehended, and there being no other evidence against him, was charged with madness and confined in Bedlam to be there treated with a low diet and beaten back into his senses.

Thus the quaint narrative ran on. Philip paused in his reading to stir the fire. This was amazingly interesting. And to think that Digley Grange had come into it. Two Gables had a real ghost! He could see the freckled face quite clearly with his mind's eye. There might almost be a freckled hand on the back of his chair if he looked round. How thrilled Ann would be. Here was romance by the bucketful!

He had come to the point where the martyr's sufferings began in real earnest: They cast him into a dungeon in the Tower. (Ann loved the Tower.) Ugh! But this was horrible! He couldn't let Ann see this. What an indescribable beast that Topcliffe the rackmaster was! James Laydon had been racked six times and otherwise tormented. These sixteenth-century narrators didn't mince matters. It was altogether too horrible and revolting. But James Laydon had remained "modestly cheerful" throughout. He had cracked his joke with the rackmaster. And when they had brought him to the gallows his pious and edifying demeanour had not prevented the joke from cropping up again. "Do thy work neatly," said James to the executioner. "I have been a neat man all my life."

He had been hanged, drawn and quartered. Philip had not realized what that meant until now—these sixteenth-century relaters were so explicit! Most decidedly he could not show this to Ann, although the story would lose immeasurably by being re-told in his own language. James's pleasant freckled face had made converts from the scaffold. They had offered him a free pardon and a benefice, if he would but acknowledge the Queen's headship of the Church (that was a curious thing to do if they had proved him guilty of plotting against her life?) but he had refused, and had died praying for the Queen and forgiving his enemies; and, as has been said, cracking his little joke with the personage who presided over the—ugh! Ann would be ill for a week if she read this about the butchering.

Chapter Five

Such was the story of James Laydon as told by contemporary documents. Philip Hallidan had encountered him, a vivid fellow-creature, over the gap of nearly four centuries. It was just as though he had actually met this young man with red hair, and a long face that belied the adjective. He could hear the hesitating speech, a kind of stutter, as he made his joke. The stammer that disappeared when he started preaching. It was queer—to put all one's money on Eternity like that. He had been as keen on religion as another fellow who isn't a fanatic is on sport, or mountaineering or that sort of thing. Well, he was a fine chap, this James Laydon, however mistaken he may have been. Ann would see that. She would see the thing in a new light now, she was so romantic; and she would back him up against Uncle Silas's preposterous demands. Ann could do pretty well anything she liked with Uncle Silas, although she had no idea of the fact.

Philip stretched out his legs towards the fire. The shadow seemed suddenly to have disappeared. The cloud between Ann and himself had been the horror, not the "terms of tenure" laid down by Uncle Silas, even if they deprived them of Two Gables. If Ann was on his side nothing else mattered.

He sat turning the little volume which had dropped from Nowhere over in his hand. The solitary feeling had gone. There seemed to be life all round, and a longing for abundant life in himself. He was wide awake, yet in a dream. Where had the book come from? What means had put him in possession of the history of James Laydon, priest? The road to Nowhere was indeed possessed of a faerie element. Richstead was haunted. No wonder it included a pied piper amongst its appurtenances. Ann had been amazingly right. Tomorrow, when he saw Ann he would be able to add the story of the mysterious appearance of the book to that of the finding of the stone. He would tell her the story of James Laydon and then everything would be right. Ann loved courage and convictions, and all that sort of thing.

Uncle Silas was less likely to treat the question as open to discussion. Philip took a long pull at his pipe—Uncle Silas was not given to going back on his word. No doubt there were difficulties ahead. But his dumps had entirely disappeared. It was queer, for the story in the book which had materialized itself on the floor of the house which was asking for a ghost was not exactly pleasant reading. Not like a love story with a happy ending. Yet it was in a way a love story—there had been the piety as well as the adventure—the hero was "in love" in his own way, and James Laydon himself evidently considered it a happy ending.

For a third time Philip went out into the empty hall. He took up the relic of the man whose personality had almost made Two Gables seem inhabited. He handled it gently. James Laydon almost seemed to be standing at his side. The stone was going to be a problem. What should he do with it?

He turned it over and read once more the words on the back:

"Return me to James Laydon."

Chapter Six

ANN WOKE UP on Sunday morning with the vague consciousness that something was wrong. The shadow which Philip had got rid of the night before lay heavy on her. Philip had said that he was a pagan, that was the thing which haunted her mind. His obstinate mood would pass, but that! Ann's idea of a non-pagan made no undue claim on the professor of that respectable cult. The Perivales were nominally "church people." Ann's mother, who had died when she was a child, had held definite views, but Dr. Perivale allowed his family to go their own way. On this particular Sunday morning Ann's fidelity to morning church-going was rewarded by a sermon on the early Christians. Ann loved the early Christians. Things mattered so much to them, and they held what was called a "mystery of Faith." She had always wished as a child that the early Christians might have continued in existence, with their Mystery of Faith; and that the entrancing entity known in the Acts of the Apostles as "the Church" had not become merely a feature of the historic past. The preacher on the present occasion was most vivid in his description of the catacombs, and the breaking of the Bread in secret places, and the guarding of the "faith once delivered to the saints." It thrilled the listener through and through. The sermon ended with a peroration congratulating the congregation on possessing a "purified religion," the adjective inferring a hiatus of alien corruption between early Christianity and the present time, to which the preacher, being a man of instinctively Christian mind, did not find it necessary to make direct reference.

The sermon sent Ann homeward in a mood which was both heroic and wistful. She felt herself pursuing the magic of the "faith once delivered to the saints." The "once" to her meant once upon a time. If only it could have meant once for all, and the Mystery of Faith be a thing of nowadays! The chief article of faith in the creed she had been brought up in seemed to be that all mystery must be excluded. It was a wonderful and enthralling Church this which had existed "once upon a time."

Philip arrived in time for mid-day dinner. Ann read his countenance eagerly as she greeted him. There was no doubt that he was in excellent form. She breathed a sigh of relief. That assertion about being a pagan was only part of his naughty temper.

As for Philip, he was bursting to tell her his news. The mystery book was there bulging in his pocket. The book that had appeared from nowhere in haunted Two Gables, which itself stood on the Road to Nowhere in haunted Richstead. Ann was to have her fill of the things which her heart loved.

Philip kept his news to himself until after dinner. The story of James Laydon was for Ann's ears alone. Tom, luckily, was too taken up with an event in the football world to make enquiries concerning the treasure-trove, and Ann had remained silent about it in the family circle. No one, fortunately, was unduly interested in Two Gables. Beryl, her married sister, who was there with her husband, was proud of the fact that they lived in hotels, and Doris, the next one, was a nurse at Bart's and too busy with her profession to enter into the details of her sister's preparations for the dull business of keeping a husband. After dinner the family would disperse and Philip would have Ann to himself, Egbert not counting.

Ann put the question directly the opportunity occurred. "You have got something to tell me," she said, making a deft opening to the subject in their minds.

"I should think I have," was the reply. "Just listen and wonder. Or would you like three guesses?"

"I would rather listen and wonder," Ann said. "Make haste, please."

"I have discovered the whole, complete and entire story of James Laydon."

Ann looked just a little scared. "Is it very dreadful?" she queried.

"Simply awful!"

"Well, then," she said, triumphantly, "now you will be ready to do what Uncle Silas wishes. Was he a very dreadful person?" She gave a little shudder. She would so much rather have had a beneficent ghost.

"He wasn't dreadful at all, he was a jolly fine fellow."

Philip checked himself. Ann's face had fallen. She tapped her foot on the floor.

"Philip!" Her eyes were alight. "You are still contrary. How could he be a fine fellow? A priest who said Mass!"

"But he was, Nan. Wait until I tell you how I came by the book."

"What book?" She broke in before he could go on. "What have you been reading?"

Philip produced the little brown volume. "He really was a splendid fellow, Nan. Let me tell you about him; and about how I came by this. It's another fairy tale of Richstead."

She gazed at him, and at the book in perplexity.

"I found it lying on the floor in the hall at Two Gables," he said. "I have no idea how it got there. It tells all about James Laydon and how he died for the religion he believed in."

Ann cast a glance of mingled fear and repulsion at the small calf-bound volume which her *fiancé* was holding out to her.

Then curiosity predominated. She put out her hand. But even as she did so the other remembered the nature of its contents. Those graphic Elizabethans! He could not allow her to read the story of Mr. James Laydon "in quartering." With a quick impulse he withdrew it and replaced it in his pocket.

She mistook the gesture. "You don't want me to read it," she said. "It is horrid." Then she added: "And I'm sure I don't want to. I wouldn't touch it with a barge pole."

She remembered a similar little calf-bound book which had come into the house once by mistake. It was called, "A mirror for devout souls," or something of the kind. Her mother had said it was a Popish book and had burnt it at once. The incident had fixed itself in her childish mind.

Her *fiancé* stood looking at her in bewilderment.

"But, Ann," he said, "you must admit it's queer, the way I found the book. The whole story of James Laydon is there, but it is frightfully harrowing, that's all."

"Of course, it would be harrowing. All about a man who forced a false religion on people, and put them on the rack."

In spite of himself Philip could not help smiling. "But Nan, dear old lady, you have got hold of entirely the wrong end of the stick. The poor beggar was put on the rack himself, and done in in the most hideous way, simply for saying Mass on that stone that we discovered yesterday."

Ann's eyes flashed. "I don't know what you mean by 'simply saying Mass,'" she said. "Mass is the most horrible idolatry."

Philip's face stiffened. "What exactly do you know about the Mass, Ann?" he asked, suddenly.

Ann might well have put it down to his habit of contrariness, or to a way he had of defending the other side when the other side was not there to defend itself, but her fears went deeper and a dreadful suspicion was fastening itself to her mind.

"What do *you* know about the Mass?" she retorted, challengingly.

"Nothing at all. That's why I object to making a cheap demonstration on my front door step."

Ann threw up her head in the manner which the novelists call queenly. She had been suddenly brought face to face with a big thing. The faith that was in her suddenly asserted itself as wearing the glamour of the faith for which the early Christians had suffered.

"Uncle Silas and I will be responsible for the 'demonstration,'" she said.

"But, Ann, if you would only read this, you would see what I am getting at."

His *fiancée* cast another glance of repulsion at the brown volume. "And you say that it dropped out of nowhere," she said. "Philip, are you making fun of me, because, I'm not altogether shallow and—pagan!"

"Ann, I'm not making fun. I simply tell you, I found this book lying in the hall, near the stone. I have no more idea how it got there than you have."

"I'm not interested in the book," she said, petulantly. "I don't understand what you are saying." Then she suddenly softened. After all, he was merely a sentimental old goose. That horrible thought that had come into her head was a mistake. "Don't be a sentimental old donkey," she said. She was mischievously turning the tables on her matter-of-fact lover.

"I suppose I am sentimental," he admitted. "But I am quite impenitent."

"So am I." Her eyes were gloriously afire. "Idols ought to be trampled on. You would have made a very poor early Christian."

"Uncle Silas doesn't understand the meaning of toleration," he retorted. "He's—a bigot."

Ann squared her neat little chin. "Toleration is cheap enough when one doesn't care," she said.

There was danger in his darkening blue eyes. "My toleration could hardly be called cheap," he reminded her. "It will cost me Two Gables, and all my prospects with Uncle Silas in business. I might not have a home to offer you."

Egbert, asleep in the arm-chair, roused up and fixed his yellow eyes first on one face then on the other.

"I suppose," Ann said, thinking it out slowly, "if I didn't marry you people would say that it was because you had not got Two Gables to offer me?"

"Undoubtedly they would."

She drew herself up. The spirit of Two Gables had got her well in its grip. "I don't care. Let them say! I could never marry anyone who was not in sympathy with my religion."

"But, Ann, I am in sympathy with all religion."

She caught him up. "Was your horrible James Laydon in sympathy with all religion?"

"He was a fine chap, Nan, he really was." He was pleading now. She was so terribly in earnest. "If you would only read this." At the worst he must let her be harrowed.

She turned her scorn on to the book. "It would all be lies," she said, with fine conclusiveness. "They were taught to tell lies." She was expounding matters declared "of faith" from the arm-chair of Uncle Silas. Then the look of fear came back into her eyes.

"Philip," she queried, "you are *sure* that you are not mixed up with these Romanists?"

She had stung him to the quick.

"Would you believe me if I told you that I am not?"

The fatal indirectness of the answer confirmed her doubts.

"I will believe you when I see the stone in its place."

The tears were standing in her eyes. Ann was in terrible

44

earnest. The lifeless thing which had hitherto been to her as the law of the land enshrined in the Statute Book was making a claim on her. She must stand up for her faith. What else was there left to stand up for if Philip loved her so little that he could put his opinions in front of her happiness?

It was feminine logic, but it was none the less potent for that.

Egbert sat and watched, rounding his owl-like eyes. There had been other courtships at Taplow Square, and lovers' tiffs had been witnessed by the negligible Egbert, but here he seemed to recognize a difference.

Philip made a last effort. "Now, look here, Ann, this is all nonsense. I'm coming along tomorrow, you know—I think I can get away all right, I've arranged it at the office."

She turned round and picked up Egbert. "You remember what Uncle Silas said. He warned us not to start getting the furniture until we had carried out his wishes."

Philip remained silent. A very square-jawed, heavy-browed Philip.

"You may come round," Ann said, "if you have done what Uncle Silas asked—and what I asked," she added, pointedly, and buried her face in Egbert's black fur.

She continued to stand with her back to him. Egbert put his paws on her shoulder and faced the disgraced lover. He liked the seat although he objected to being used as a pocket-handkerchief. On the whole, he decided not to purr.

"Well, Ann, I must be off now."

"Very well. Good-bye."

He went over and shook Egbert's paw. "Say 'good-bye' for me, old bean," he said. He dared not say any more. He dreaded the repulse. The unthinkable thing had happened. He and Ann had quarrelled.

Ann did not let go of Egbert until after she had heard the front door close. Philip had gone. She had hurt him and he had hurt her. It is one thing to have theories and stick to them in debating societies, and all that, but it was cruel and selfish of him to insist on going against Uncle Silas like this unless—but, no, she could safely set that fear aside. At the worst he had told Uncle Silas that he was a pagan.

The *ting* of the telephone bell interrupted her line of thought. It was generally Ann's business to answer the 'phone. It was Uncle Silas calling. Rather an ominous Uncle Silas. Was his nephew at Taplow Square? No?—Ah, it was Ann speaking. Uncle Silas sounded very cross. He must have been beguiled to a high celebration in the morning; or, perhaps his protest speech for the election run on an anti-ritualistic issue had not gone down well afterwards. Poor Uncle Silas.

"Is there any message?" Ann asked.

"No—yes. You may tell Philip that I am returning to town the first thing Tuesday morning. I will be coming through Richstead on the car and will pick him up. What? He has arranged to spend tomorrow night in London at his rooms? Well, never mind, tell him that he can leave me a message on the garden path. Good-bye."

Ann set down the receiver. At the other end of the line Mr. Bulkington did the same. It was not possible to transmit a grim and sardonic smile along the telephone—a more scientific age may achieve that—and, after all, it was Ann and not the recalcitrant nephew at the other end.

Chapter Seven

PHILIP SPENT the rest of the day at his club. He was half a mind not to return to Two Gables at all that night. The beastly place gave him the creeps. The whole business was so preposterous. They had fallen out over a matter that neither of them cared a pin about. Ann had never got anything out of the cut-and-dried church services they had attended together on Sundays. And here was he defying Uncle Silas in defence of a superstition, or, rather, of a relic of a superstition; and Ann bristling up like a second Uncle Silas, with a brief for the glorious Reformation. It was altogether too ridiculous. Yet, if it was merely ridiculous the remedy was at hand. He had only to put the stone of contention into its place and he and Ann would be off choosing their Elizabethan chairs and tables. What a fantastic business it was!

He finally decided to return to Two Gables. He could put in a good morning's work before breakfast, and the time was getting short. Of course, Nan had been right to expect him to give in. No doubt it was the giving in that had stuck in his gorge. Poor little Nankin, she was but the victim of her upbringing.

Two Gables appeared ghostlier than ever to its custodian when late that night he let himself into the gaunt, square hall. What a queer, fantastic place it was, with its mixture of reality and make-believe. Even the real bits were only part of a fake—except the stone, that was real!—and the ghost of James Laydon. James Laydon had been such a remarkably real person.

He could feel him about now, taking stock of what was going on, and see the puckers gathering under his greeny-grey eyes as he surveyed with amusement the chairs and tables from Crampton's. This James Laydon pervaded the place!

He turned into his room, switched the light on and set light to the fire, although he meant to get straight into bed. The place was chilly. It would be better when the furniture was in. Crampton's was undoubtedly the place; and they mustn't miss that Sale.

Best get to sleep at once and end this fool of a day. So thought Philip. But sleep was elusive. He lay awake, tossing and brooding over the ugly fact that he and Ann had not parted friends. He had better get something to read. But there was nothing but "Missionary Priests." Well, "Missionary Priests" might do the job; and it might qualify his opinion of the class, as sampled in James Laydon who was no doubt an exception. Taken as a whole they would probably be a dull and not attractive set.

But "Missionary Priests" did not prove a good bedside book, since the office of a bedside book is to summon gentle sleep. Neither did it fulfil the other requisition. An hour and a half later Philip was still wide-awake, and still reading. There were dozens of such stories as James Laydon's. First he had read mechanically; then it had got a grip on him. The picture of the times was so vivid, the homeliness of the detail so human. Men rose out of the pages who might be living today. And such men! Some were priests who converted men by their charity and meekness; some were laymen who could double a fist in defence of their faith and if necessary "break the heads" of the Queen's pursuivants when they appeared on the scene. The power of wit and repartee recorded of others made the account of their disputations with their judges uncommonly spicy reading. They certainly had their wits about them. Philip, in short, found much to extenuate the deeply religious *motif* of the book which was robbing him of his sleep. These were human beings—sportsmen who played a game which set the senses a-tingling. Men who held a great secret which made them laugh at death. For them, at any rate, the road went on, to Somewhere.

Philip dropped his book, switched off the light, and fell to thinking. There had been an attendant marvel to this marvel of mirth in suffering. It was the hatred which these men had encountered from the enemies of their Faith. An insensate hatred, fear, and detestation. Precisely the same as that which functioned in Uncle Silas in the present day in regard to all things that savoured of Popery. And Ann's unreasoned attitude was to be accounted for in the same way. This "phobia" was a psychological freak, a kind of ancestral complex which he had run to earth in the history of three and a half centuries ago. The "popery" of today proved its continuity with the Popery of the Elizabethan missioners by the existence of this "corporate complex." Poor Uncle Silas!

As sleep overcame him, Philip found himself saying, "Righto, James Laydon, I'll play up."

Then he really did go to sleep.

Next morning Philip woke betimes. The sun was streaming in the window. He became conscious as he stretched himself that the day before him contained some big issue. What was it? This was Monday, the day when he was to go with Ann and choose the furniture, unless the wretched office rung him up at the last moment. Was that the big issue?—Choosing the right chairs and tables? No, there was something else. The miserable business of James Laydon's stone, and Uncle Silas's proviso. He had got to get it into its place before he set out to fetch Ann. Ann had been very annoyed with him yesterday, and he had played the goat. Well—they would do the Sale after Crampton's.

The mistletoe-bough chest would be going cheap at the Sale. Crampton's Elizabethan settles were quite good. He got up and dressed. He would do a bit of gardening before breakfast.

He went out of the front door to get a breath of the morning air. The first thing that met his eye was the gap in the path. The two carved heads on either side of the porch, the wooden grotesques which had so enchanted Ann, were watching him. They wept and laughed. The stone which Mr. Bulkington had dislodged still lay on the side of the path. "I must tidy it up," Philip told himself, grimly.

He returned indoors. But Two Gables was determined not to give him any peace. Digley Grange cried out at him from every corner. He took refuge in his caretaker's room with its banal modernities, but on the floor, where he had kicked it off the bed during the night, lay "Memoirs of Missionary Priests."

Then he remembered that he had promised James Laydon to play up.

It appeared to be a peculiarity of Two Gables that it possessed daylight ghosts. The sunshine which was pouring through the diamond panes of the dining-room window by no means eliminated the picture of James Laydon's cloaked figure approaching up the garden path with his proscribed kit concealed under his arm. It fitted in all right with the other everyday things. James Laydon was stupendously ordinary, as ordinary as the milkman. He seemed to be all over the place, and finding much entertainment in the importance of Elizabethan chairs and cabinets. He might even be poking fun at the present occupier—this man with a freckled face who stammered when he wasn't preaching.

A shabby man with hand-bills came up the path and deposited one in the letter slot. As he walked away he caught his heel in the gap where, had the stone but been in its place, he could have taken a non-heroic measure to stamp out popery. Mr.

Bulkington's nephew turned his back on the diamond panes. There was plenty of time. He would go to the back and dig a bit—turn over the potato patch.

Philip worked at the potato patch. Then he came in and made his breakfast. It was nearly time to start out and fetch Ann. He must see to the stone business. It was an ugly one, but what could he do? He went out into the front garden and surveyed the gap.

"Do thy work neatly." Was it James Laydon whispering the words into his mental ear? It would be in irony, not in jest. The owner of the stone of sacrifice could have jested over the desecration of his own mortal parts, but not at this act of sacrilege.

It might, indeed be a mocking spirit. The devil would doubtless be amused at the sight of Mr. Bulkington's "creature" securing for himself the pseudo-glories of Two Gables at the expense of a long cherished conviction that—"hang it! whatever he was he was not a cad."

"D—d—do thy work neatly." He could even hear the stammer!

Philip went into the hall and stood before the Tudor mantelpiece. He picked up the stone. The five crosses were distinctly marked on it. There is something compelling about the sacred symbol of Redemption (for all that Uncle Silas subscribed to a society which engaged in the destruction of crucifixes as one of its pious works); pagan that he was, it had its effect on Philip. He replaced the stone on the ledge, and taking the cigarette out of his mouth stood regarding it thoughtfully. It was the first piece of antique furniture which they had acquired. Certainly genuine; and if it hadn't served to furnish the house it had done more, it had populated it!

Then it was that something caught his eye, lying on the ground. He was not sorry for the distraction. Another mysterious materialization? It was a sheet of paper this time. He picked it up and ran his eye over it. It was a leaflet announcing that Richstead was to be favoured with the presentation of a film at its Picture House, entitled: "The Black Plotters."

Obviously, it had come through the letter slot. As there was as yet no box to receive it, it lay on the ground. The next moment he was calling himself names. Idiot! Ass! Here was the obvious solution of the mystery of the appearance of the book. Someone must have put it through the letter slot, and in opening the hall door he had pushed it aside so that it lay in the corner and did not suggest its mode of entry. Two Gables must be a queer place to bemuse a man's wits like this. No wonder Ann had been unable to believe him and had thought that he was pulling her leg, or inventing outrageous fables. He glanced at the paper in his hand. "The Black Plotters." Richstead no doubt would flock obediently to its Cinema to be thrilled, but black plotters were rather lost on him! "My black plotters hunt me down in the sanctity of my home," Philip thought, grimly.

But the mystery of the book, so far as the ownership was concerned, and the hand which had pushed it through the letter box remained. It was sufficiently intriguing, even if the preternatural had been eliminated. Philip crumpled up the paper in his hand. He was in the toils of a plot, the victim of coincidence. No wonder Ann had been bewildered.

"Let me see," Philip said to himself, "what did I come out here for?"

What had he come there for? To fetch the stone of sacrifice and set it in its place, where the tradesman's tout would trample it with his heel. That had got to be done before he went and trafficked in the "let's pretend" antiquities at Crampton's.

He stood there for another minute or so; then he went out into the garden and seized his spade. He went round and did things to the rockery. The avenue was exuding its quota of citizens of day-time London. They emerged from their gates and headed for the station, down the avenue. The City would return them punctually at night. It was a peculiarly circular existence, this on the road to Nowhere!

By rights Philip ought to have been one of them, for although he had got off from business, he was due to be calling at Taplow Square for Ann. As it was he stood, coatless with his shirt-sleeves rolled up, mopping his brow and watching them as he leant on his spade. Suppose the pied piper were to come along and entice all the money-makers in the other direction, along the road to Somewhere. They would all miss their train, and they would all spend the day with Nature, as he intended to do. He was no longer in a position to invest in expensive furniture; and Uncle Silas might thank him for thus disinterestedly adding to the value of his property.

Eleven o'clock still found Philip digging for dear life among the cabbage beds. Digging is a fine occupation for a man who doesn't want to think. Ann would be looking out for him. His non-arrival would settle the question, they had agreed on that. He need not 'phone. Besides, he was not sure what was going to happen—was happening? Ann would interpret his non-appearance in the only possible way. If the old office had sent him an S.O.S., of course, he would have rung her up. She would know by now that he had refused to give in. That he was either an avowed Romanist with an indulgenced lie on the tip of his tongue, or a pig-headed fellow who would not yield his opinion in a minor matter for the sake of the woman he pretended to care for. He was a pig-headed fellow, he knew, but, hang it! this was not pig-headedness.

Two Gables had taken an uncanny revenge on the client of the Road to Nowhere and become Digley Grange with all its concomitant parts!

Chapter Eight

A S FOR ANN, she woke on Monday morning to a world from which the bottom was in imminent danger of being knocked out. This was the day which was to prove if Philip really loved her; or if she had merely dreamed an ideal Philip—she was such a dreamer—a Philip who was constitutionally incapable of deception, or of ignoble sympathies. A Philip who really loved her and had not merely drifted into an engagement with her in the nature of things because they had known each other from babies.

It is not pleasant to face a world from which the bottom has been knocked out. Love, besides making the world go round, supplies it with a good solid ground for one to stand on. Whilst love is there, nothing else matters vitally. Even separation is a thing which deals only with the present and future, it still leaves a substantial past for the feet to cling to by means of sweet and tender memories; but disillusionment is complete annihilation. If Philip did not put in his appearance today—if he had not done the simple thing she required of him, then Philip had never so much as existed. This "stranger" might be mixed up with the enemies of liberty and truth. He would be someone with a twisted conscience that permitted him to tell lies; or, and that was a terrible thought, he might be someone who had no particular interest in the girl he was going to marry except that his old Uncle was rather fond of her!

Ann lived the morning through in a pitiable state of nervous tension. When no Philip appeared she played up bravely to the others. He had not been able to get the day off, after all. She recalled that there had been a possibility of this and so saved her conscience from the fib. But if that had been the case he would have telephoned. A forlorn hope presented itself for Ann to snatch at:

Philip might be sulking? He might have been sent for to the office and, just to indulge his outraged feelings, for they would be outraged if he had been obliged to climb down and do as he was told, he might have let her think, for a day, that it was the other reason. It would not be unlike Philip, he hated climbing down, silly old thing!

A forlorn hope is sometimes a more impelling thing than one founded on a stronger premise. It can impel to action from the fact that the person harbouring a forlorn hope is generally one by the circumstances of the case afflicted with the fidgets. Unrest, inability to sit down and wait, caused Ann to give entertainment to the notion that came to her on this the wretchedest afternoon of her life. If Philip had climbed down he would have put the stone into its place before he left for the office (Ann was certain now that the office *had* summoned Philip), for he would not be returning to Two Gables that evening. He was spending the night at his own place, and Uncle Silas had got to find his message waiting for him. Why not run over to Richstead and see for herself? Philip need never know. It would set her mind at rest. She had the afternoon at her disposal, and at any rate it was better than doing nothing.

It was a very forlorn, and yet, withal, hopeful, Ann whom the 'bus set down at the foot of the Road to Nowhere. She had held a brief sturdily all the way along for her theory regarding Philip's behaviour, and the self-convinced are docile converts to the theory imposed by the desire of the heart. Philip had set the stone in its place and then he had gone to work, either from necessity or perhaps because he was just a little sulky. Climbing down is a feat which brings no athletic joys with it, the descent of Everest, if one comes to think of it, is never billed or made the subject of headlines.

Richstead somehow looked very different today. The piper was not in his usual place. The pedestrians were footing it decorously. Ann turned up the avenue, with its air of concrete well-being. Yet once again Two Gables "hit her in the eye" with its unexpectedness. It looked more exotic than ever. More unreal and dream-like. Yet Two Gables was terribly real. Was that a face at the window? How imaginative she was!

Ann felt her heart stand still as she stood at the gate. The pathway twisted round towards the porch where the faces would be watching the impending drama. She had to enter and walk a little way before she could get a view of the fateful spot.

The next minute she was gazing at a gap in the path—in the centre, where people trod. The carved heads were smiling and weeping. A mocking smile and a crocodile tear.

Ann stood there, her soul in combat with an overweening desire to give in. Philip had been roped in by these awful people, the idea was infinitely more supportable than the other. He could not help himself. He had put off obeying Uncle Silas, forgetting that it was his last chance. He might be coming back tonight?—still the sulky Philip—and then it would not be too late.

She glanced at the long, low window to the left of the mocking porch, whose diamond panes played tricks with the present-day vision. *There was a face there!* And it was a familiar one—Philip's! He had been watching all the while. He had not gone to the office. He was watching now, seeing how she would take it!

All Ann's semi-exhausted "manhood" returned to her. Had she not got principles to stand by as well as he? She and Uncle

Silas were iconoclasts. She was going to hold out, as the early Christians had done. Two Gables had entoiled her in its aura.

She flung herself round on her heel. On either side the graven images of the presiding spirit wept and smiled, effectively covering the situation.

.   .   .   .   .

But to return to Philip:

At twelve o'clock Philip walked down to the Broadway and bought a loaf of bread and some cheese, and a bottle of ale. Then he went back and settled himself in the caretaker's room to feed.

He had not faced the Bull Hotel, that blithering old piper was piping in front of it and it gave him the hump. Hard fare, moreover, suited his mood. If only Ann had been sharing the bread and cheese with him. If she had seen the thing from his point of view she might have been willing to share bread and cheese and do without Uncle Silas's subsidy to their marriage arrangements.

"Bah!" He was getting cynical. He must go out and do some more digging. James Laydon could find nothing to smile at in bread and cheese and the cabbage patch. For the time being he was on excellent terms with the freckled adventurer whose engaging weakness was idolatry.

He went out, a giant refreshed, and dug strenuously. A day off from the office was an admirable thing now and again. If he had shown up there it would have involved explanations.

Philip came in at tea-time and put on his kettle. He was beginning to feel rather fagged. If only Nan had been there to preside over the kettle. How dismal the place was! No wonder Ann wasn't there. She would be feeling most horribly hurt. Why on earth was he playing the goat like this? By now she would have confirmed her conviction that he was a Papist in disguise, or an utterly impossible prig. He made his tea with water that had boiled after a fashion. He really was rather done up. He had made a beastly mess of things—no, not the garden, he had done that work neatly enough. . . . He believed he could hear that confounded piper in the distance. He would go out and give him sixpence to clear off.

So Philip's thoughts rambled on as he drank his parboiled tea. Thank goodness, he was going to town tonight, he simply couldn't stand another night in this place. He would shake the dust of Two Gables off his feet for good and all.

Suddenly he heard the sound of the click of the garden gate. Was it that beastly old piper come to ask for a copper? He went over and glanced out of the window. He stood staring, as though his eyes were belying him. It was Nan! Nan herself! She was making her way up the path with her eyes fixed searchingly on the ground. She was looking to see if he had done his work neatly. But she was here. She had come to look for him. He would be able to make her understand. Nan was here. That was the main thing. Two Gables had lost all its bogeys at one fell swoop! She had reached the turn in the path by the rockery. Before her eyes was yawning the ominous gap in the paving. He seemed rooted to the spot. Ann was looking up now. Their eyes met. She had seen him, but there was no greeting in her gaze, only a kind of horror. She stood stock still, there, with the gap between her and the doorstep. She was looking at the path again, then back at him. He realized that his presence there would be an additional affront. But he stood as rooted to the spot.

For a minute Philip stood there. Then he saw the anguish in the little white face. It was too much! There was nothing for it. He would give her the stone to do what she would with. It would be his greeting. Ann was standing out there waiting to be let in.

He darted out into the hall. The stone was reposing in its place. He tried to seize hold of it, but his arms hung limp beside him. She, Ann, would take the stone from him and put it in its place, to be trodden on by the touts and callers, and general traffickers on the road to Nowhere. Ann, the dreamer of dreams, the idealist—the kindred spirit of these men who held a vision in their eyes. Not if he knew it! Neither should it be said of her that she had caused him to act—like a cad. Ann!

He turned from the mantelpiece empty-handed and went and opened the door. She was walking away down the path.

"Ann," he called, "Ann!"

She turned round. An imperious, silent, statuesque Ann. She was pointing at the gap.

What could he say?

He stood there, speechless.

She waited a long moment. Then she deliberately turned on her heel again. He watched her walking away. Then he cried, once more: "Ann!"

But she had clicked the gate and gone.

Should he run after her? It was not too late. But he must not go empty-handed.

Philip returned into the hall. He stood before the stone of contention. The temptation was surging up to cease "playing the goat" and sacrificing Ann to this quixotic notion of his. There was but one thing for it—he must get rid of the stone. But how? His eyes fell on the words, "Return me to James Laydon." They seemed to read like a mandate as well as an answer to his question. But who were James Laydon's executors? his trustees? He supposed any Roman Catholic priest would do. He pressed his forehead against the edge of the shelf that held the stone of sacrifice. "All right," he said out loud, as though James Laydon, with his freckled face, might have been standing there to hear him. Then he went off and scoured his hands. He didn't want to look like a tramp. He fetched his attaché case. It took the stone quite comfortably. Poor little Nannikin. Would she ever condescend to ask him what he had done with the stone? Would she ever speak to him again? Would she believe that he had really cared for her? If she only did that it would be something.

The policeman at the end of the Avenue was able to inform Philip where a Roman Catholic church was to be found. There was St. Joseph's down towards the station, and another at New Park. A Catholic church right enough although it was queer calling it the "Church of the English Martyrs," seeing that the martyrs were all Protestants. It could be reached by walking over the common, or by taking a couple of 'buses.

Philip thanked the constable and went in search of a taxi. The second church attracted him because of its name. If James Laydon could be said to possess a terrestrial address it would surely be: c/o the Church of the English Martyrs. "Return me to James Laydon" had not been such an impossible command after all.

Chapter Nine

HE REVEREND Timothy Saunders was not unpardon-
ably proud of the fact that Richstead New Park, for
all that it was a new district, and but a working man's
colony at that, possessed a Catholic church of its own. The
church had been built owing to Father Timothy's untiring
efforts, though it is only just to acknowledge that these had
been munificently aided by his friend, Mr. Duncan Rolt, a convert who had made some money in America. It was a curious
structure. The space available had run to length rather than
breadth, and the architect had adapted his scheme with some
ingenuity to the restriction. The church was a long vaulted
building with a subtle suggestion of a crypt about it. The pro-
portions were arranged to accentuate the length rather than
modify it. The local paper, when it described a function, as it
sometimes did, always alluded to the "distant sanctuary"—
sometimes it was, "dim and distant," rendering homage to the
architect's skill.

The church was dedicated to the English Martyrs, to whom
its main benefactor always declared that he owed his conver-
sion. On the afternoon on which I propose to introduce the
reader of this comedy to Father Timothy Saunders (an Irish
mother had chosen his first name and an English father had
handed on the other) the good priest was expecting a visitor in
the shape of the above-named friend and benefactor. Duncan
Rolt might turn up now at any moment. It was some years since

he had been to England and it would be a merry meeting for the two friends.

It was for this reason that the announcement made by Hannah, Father Timothy's housekeeper-factotum, that there was a gentleman in the waiting-room asking for the father was hailed with an alacrity which did not always follow a summons of the kind. Hannah's "gentlemen" as often as not came in search of monetary assistance, any sum from sixpence upwards being acceptable, and generally forthcoming. On this occasion history seemed to be about to repeat itself, for the gentleman in waiting was not the one expected. He was a complete stranger, and he had an attaché case in his hand, which was ominous. Father Saunders cast a swift glance at the attaché case and drew a conclusion from past experience. He was a young man with a pleasant countenance enough, and quite well dressed. No doubt he had got something to sell for the firm he represented in the case. He was evidently new to his job, and didn't much relish it for he blushed when he introduced himself, and glanced furtively at the case in his hand.

Father Tim followed the glance and helped him out.

"Well?" he said. "What have you got there?"

The direct question, if it surprised the visitor certainly helped him on.

"It's an Elizabethan altar stone," he replied, tersely. "No, I'm not wanting to offer it for sale." He interrupted the other's expression of countenance. "Here is my name." He placed a card in the padre's hand. "A relative of mine," he continued, "has just purchased a house in Richstead Common Avenue and I am acting as caretaker whilst it is being put in order. It is a reconstructed Tudor manor house, and all the timber is sixteenth century. It came from Digley, in Xshire."

"Digley!" Father Saunders echoed. "Let me see, that's connected with one of the English martyrs." He was all attention now.

"Yes, James Laydon; his name is on the stone I have here. It was discovered hidden in an old oak beam which had been hollowed out to make a hiding place."

"Goodness me! This is remarkably interesting, Mr.—er—Hallidan." Father Saunders read the name of the visitor on the card in his hand.

The other was taking something out of the case, which he had set down on the table. "Here it is," he said, "I fancied it might be of more interest to you than to me."

The priest took the stone. He held it reverently in his hands. He examined it closely. He looked up. There was moisture in his eyes. Then he spoke.

"And you found this hidden away in an old beam?"

"I can vouch for the hiding-place. I was there when it was brought to light. I had no idea what it was, of course."

"Then you are not a Catholic?"

The question provoked a rather peculiar smile.

"Oh, dear no. I'm a pagan."

"Then it is extraordinarily good of you to be doing this." The padre eyed the pagan with the warmest approval. "You realize what such a thing means to us Catholics?"

"I think I do—in a fashion." The pagan said it rather drily. "When my uncle—the house is his—explained what it was I felt that you might have more use for it than I should."

The priest reflected. "Then the house belongs to your uncle? Pardon me, but you just spoke of the stone being no use to you, yourself."

The other explained, rather gruffly: "It was to have been passed on to me. I am getting married—I was to have been married." Why did the wretched man ask questions. He was anxious to get the business over and be off.

The priest spoke again. "Then the stone is really the property of your uncle. I presume he has no use for it either?"

The reply was given with a very sardonic smile.

"He suggested that I should use it for the crazy paving on the path."

"Heavens, what a ghastly idea!" The other drew in his breath. "You, of course, didn't wish to do that."

A shrug of the shoulders. The visitor was rather an off-hand young man, or was it that he was trying to be a rather off-hand young man? The priest gave a shrewd glance at the frank countenance, to which he had taken a strong liking.

"I don't quite see things eye to eye with my uncle," was the rather bored reply. "He's Silas Bulkington, the M.P., you know."

"Good gracious!" the padre cried. "Why, Popery is his tame bogey. He takes it about with him everywhere—his notion of Popery I mean. It's a sort of Bonzo, a fabulous creature with exploits to its credit. He wouldn't approve of your passing the stone on to me. I hope I am not going to get you into trouble, my boy?" The priest's kindly eyes were full of concern.

The reply was irresistible. Philip Hallidan never had been able to resist a repartee.

"You can't," he said. "I am in trouble already."

The other's face lengthened. He waited for more in silent sympathy. His visitor had let himself in for an explanation. It might just as well be a full one.

"My uncle is annoyed with me for not using the stone as he suggested," he said. "He made it a condition of my occupying the house after I was married. I was afraid I might knuckle under if the stone remained in my possession, so I brought it along to you."

The priest listened to this somewhat emasculated version of the story. He watched the speaker whose face, he noted, was haggard and drawn, and took measures to fill in the gaps.

"And what does your *fiancée* say to it?" he enquired.

The other reddened. "She is very angry with me."

"She dislikes Catholics, too?"

"She hates—my uncle's Bonzo—she doesn't know anything about Catholics. Neither do I, for matter of that, but I just happened to read something about this James Laydon in an old book I got hold of, and it didn't make me extra anxious to insult his convictions."

"What book was that?"

"I believe I've got it here"—he was feeling in his pocket. "Yes, here it is."

Father Saunders turned the little volume over in his hand: "Ah, yes, Challoner. I see it is old Carlyon's copy. So you know him?"

"I should be glad to know who Carlyon is," was the answer. "I found the book lying inside the hall-door at Two Gables. It had come through the letter-slot. I haven't a notion who Carlyon is."

The priest laughed. "You have been making friends with the piper," he said, "without learning his name. A great many people do that."

"The piper?"

"Yes, Carlyon is his name. He's the old fellow who plays a pipe on the Broadway. He's a grand Catholic, a saint all but the halo. I could tell you his story if you had time to hear it. He has suffered for his faith, too. What he doesn't know about the English Martyrs isn't history."

Philip Hallidan sat reflecting. He was thoroughly intrigued. The entrance of the piper into the mystery was most bewildering.

"I know the old piper," he said, "but I have only spoken to him once and it was not about religion. Ann, my *fiancée*, took a fancy to him and nicknamed him the 'pied piper.'"

The priest was thoroughly interested.

"Your *fiancée* hasn't cultivated his acquaintance and told him about the stone?" he suggested.

Philip shook his head. "We told no one except—wait a bit. I've got it! He must have overheard us when we were telling Ann's brother about it. We met him on the Broadway, and, of course, that was it—the old piper was standing near and he must have overheard us."

The mystery of the book which had dropped from space had suddenly been combed out. The simplest of natural explanations had presented itself. But it was still uncanny—the pied piper having a hand in it. What would Ann say to that? She would regard the piper for the future as a prophet of "Bonzo," if indeed she had anything to say. He had forgotten!

"Just like Carlyon," Father Saunders said, laughing. "He would be too much of a gentleman to eavesdrop, but out on the Broadway one listens without thinking. His hearing is extra sharp to make up for his want of speech."

"He makes that up on his pipe, doesn't he?"

The other nodded. "Quite true. He prays on his pipe, that old fellow. He is a great man of prayer is Carlyon. He lost his speech some years ago from shock, but the wisdom in his head isn't the kind that can express itself in words. All the mystics are dumb folk."

The speaker pulled himself up, remembering that he was addressing one of the other sheep; but his hearer was interested.

"Ann thought he was a kind of magician," he said. And with that he found himself telling his new friend the story of the road to Nowhere; and of the pied piper who led the bewitched inhabitants of Suburbia up the road to the Never-never Land. It was Ann's fancy and Ann was very present in his mind. He took sick comfort in speaking of things which pertained to her.

The other listened with gratifying attention. "Your *fiancée* must have a very penetrating mind," he said. "A very delightful lady she must be."

Philip capitulated. This appreciative padre was henceforth as one of his most intimate friends. He had taken Ann's dream-stuff in a way that made it almost seem real. He took him into his confidence, once for all.

"I am not sure that she is my *fiancée* any longer," he said, ruefully. "She won't forgive me for not giving in to Uncle Silas. *She* made it a condition, too. She's got the 'no-popery' complex as well as my uncle, she can't understand that it is simply that I don't want to be a cad."

Father Saunders laid his hand on the shoulder of the young man who had been so wrongfully suspected of having truck with Catholicism. "It is hard luck," he said. "I understand your motive perfectly. I for my part"—he smiled—"don't suspect you of Roman tendencies, except that the heroes of our Faith were men who had particular dislike to 'being cads.' We must pray that it comes right. I will ask Carlyon to pray. He may be in the church now, by the way. He usually pays it a visit in the evening."

"Well," Philip said, rising and looking for his hat, "I have returned his property to James Laydon's trustees. I fancy they have more right to it than my uncle."

"I think I agree with you," the priest said, smiling. He led the way to the door, and paused. "You might perhaps like a peep at our church," he said. "We have an altar of the English martyrs where your stone will probably be placed. And you may see old Carlyon. He won't be piping his prayers in church, but he often does on his way over here."

Philip accepted the invitation. He could hardly have declined without discourtesy. "The church will be rather dark, I'm afraid," Father Timothy apologized. He was right. The church boasted only of one light in addition to the sanctuary lamp. It looked curiously cave-like and filled with mystery. Philip glanced round him. A few votive candles were doing their best to make darkness visible before a shrine. It was that of the English martyrs. Father Saunders paused in front of it.

"It is here that we commemorate James Laydon," he said, "along with the other martyrs."

Philip read the words inscribed on the altar. "Blessed English Martyrs, pray for us." It was here that Catholics would come to get into touch with the owner of the stone. It was here that would be carried out the behest engraved on it: "return me to James Laydon." It was all most bewilderingly queer.

"It has already got its altar-stone," the priest was explaining. "You see, every altar has its consecrated stone, marked with the five wounds of Christ. The wounds in His hands and feet, and the wound in His heart. Whether it be the high altar at St. Peter's in Rome or the rigged-up altar on the battlefield, or the ancient altar in the catacombs where they said Mass, as you know, on the tombs of the Christian martyrs. Everywhere it is the same Mystery of Faith."

They moved away in silence. The priest paused as they crossed the nave and genuflected towards the altar in the distance. The tabernacle curtains were draped on either side of its golden gate. It was a large, handsome tabernacle and the light from the sanctuary lamp was reflected on the burnished portal. There were dim figures kneeling near them. They were standing at the back of the church. "We keep the Blessed Sacrament there," the priest said. "People who have received Holy Communion in the morning sometimes like to come back and say, 'thank You' later on in the day. And others," he added, "like to come and find eternity just beyond the little gate yonder."

He glanced round. He had promised to introduce his visitor to the piper. But at that moment they were interrupted. Hannah in a great flutter, had pursued the priest with a message. The expected visitor had arrived.

"Pardon me," Father Saunders said, "if I leave you now—but," the thought struck him, "perhaps I might introduce you to my friend as the donor of the altar-stone. He will be most extraordinarily interested in it. He is a great client of the English martyrs."

But Philip excused himself. He didn't feel quite up to the rôle of benefactor. "Another day, perhaps?" Father Saunders said. "I shall have a great story to tell my friend tonight, if I may do so without breaking your confidence?"

"I don't mind," Philip said. "I would rather you told the piper, he might pipe a prayer for me."

"Of course, I should like to tell Carlyon. He had a hand in it." The priest held his own hand out. "Good-bye, my boy. God bless and reward you. Let me know the end of the story."

Philip crossed over to the shrine of the English Martyrs. His form of address was not couched in the terms found in the prayer-books, with an indulgence attached.

"Well, James Laydon," he said, rather defiantly, "I've played up. About the least you can do is to pray for me."

Chapter Ten

LOVERS' QUARRELS are usually the most unreasonable and avoidable of all quarrels. When Ann turned herself out of the precincts of Two Gables the *genius loci* who presided over the ordered doings of the inmates of the Tower House and its neighbours would neither have laughed nor cried, it would simply have been bored by the recurrence of the usual thing. Engaged couples invariably come to words over the question of furnishing.

But there the genius of the Tower House and The Oaks would have erred. Ann as she closed the gate resolutely behind her, with the clang that Philip would hear and interpret, was conscious that the trouble went deeper than a mere dispute—even a dispute for conscience sake. Had she arrived at the conclusion that Philip was a Papist in disguise, at any rate something would have remained—the sense of having acted on principle and suffered for her Faith; but the fear that held her heart and squeezed it in a vice was a growing conviction that this was in no sense a "lovers' quarrel" from the simple fact that Philip had never really been her lover. He had brought himself up on the notion that he had got to marry her, and Uncle Silas had always favoured the idea. He had always gone to great lengths to please Uncle Silas, but this affair of the stone had been the last straw and he had taken the opportunity to shake himself free from—everything.

For all these years she had been following a road to Nowhere.

Ann headed her way along—the sooner she got home the better. The adored Philip of the past, the chivalrous, adoring Philip, was but an occupant of the Never-never Land. If only it lay beyond the common how gladly she would go there instead of home by 773 motor 'bus.

The train of her thought was suddenly arrested. She had been dragging her leaden feet along the road-away-from-Philip; and, half dazed with misery, she had not noticed whither it was leading. There in front of her lay the Never-never Land! Richstead Common, not the Broadway, was spreading its lure in front of the dreamer of vain dreams. She had made identically the same mistake as she and Philip had made on that first occasion. The original false impression had asserted itself again in her preoccupied mind. The irony of it was too cruel. They had been so egregiously happy that day only a week ago. And they had been looking forward to exploring the common and the country beyond.

She stood gazing vaguely in front of her. No, she was not going to turn back and retrace her steps. It would mean passing Two Gables again, and that was more than she could bear. How could she pass it without rushing in and asking him to love her just a little? She would just walk on and on and on.

The common possessed a very definite lure. There was a narrow track threading its way between the gorse and blackberry bushes. Beyond that, clumps of trees rose darkly. Beyond them, again, would be the open country stretching away to the hills and vales of Xshire. It looked lonely and fearsome. As she stood there hesitating, a sound fell on her ear. "Oh, it was too bad!" There was the old piper again. He was playing that same tune which he had played the other day on the Broadway when he had set her feet a-jogging. The shopman had said that he lived somewhere on the common. He must be a kind of hermit.

She caught sight of his figure in the distance. The impulse came to her; she would follow him and see what happened. It might be the road to Nowhere, or to the elusive Never-never Land, which was the same thing. She had been so persistent that it was a road to Somewhere. Well, the spell of the pied piper was anyhow preferable to the one cast over Philip by the sinister associations of Two Gables. He really must be under a spell. Perhaps he really had been hypnotized by those Papists and she was really making a sacrifice for her faith!

The tune in the distance served to hasten Ann's footsteps. It was tender and soothing. Yes, she would follow on and see where it led to.

The common was very lonely. There was nobody in sight except the pied piper. His note was intermittent. Every now and again he played a snatch of an air, sometimes merry, some-times plaintive. They were in the midst of the undergrowth now. Ann began to get just a little uncomfortable. It was too late to turn back. The afternoon was fading into twilight, and there was protection in the figure going on ahead. The common was horribly wild and lonely. Sooner or later they must come to some human habitation. A village with a railway station, or per-haps one of those 'buses which run right out into the country? She had lessened the distance between herself and her leader. She kept close behind him now. They were approaching what appeared to be a wood. The old piper was playing a hymn tune. She fitted the words to it from the hymn-book which they used at church. It was one of those hymns which gave her strange feelings of a Never-never Land in religion. Someone had told her that it was a translation of a very ancient hymn.

> "Deep in His heart for us
>   The wound of love He bore;
>   That love which He enkindles still
>   In hearts which Him adore."

Surely it must be the wounded love in her own heart that made the words seem so poignant? Her heart was as heavy as a stone. A wounded stone, that was what her heart felt like.

Nervous strain was beginning to tell on her. The road to Nowhere was haunted by dark shadows. Where was she being led to? The path they were pursuing lay right through the wood. As they got nearer, Ann seemed to discern white, waving forms beyond the first belt of trees. She drew in her breath. What was it?

The next moment the question was answered. The wood, which had thought better of being a wood, or even a plantation, after the single belt of trees ended abruptly. In a bare open space beyond was stretched a long line of white garments hanging out to dry, and beyond the open space was a long and appallingly ugly building, above which was paraded the legend:

"Richstead New Park Laundry."

With the laundry, Richstead Common ended.

On the fringe lay a net-work of small yellow houses, newly built—a dreadful recurrence of the London which Ann had fondly imagined she had left behind. It was slum Suburbia in one of its most utilitarian moods.

Relief was decidedly the feeling uppermost in Ann's mind. The pied piper had been playing a pretty prank on her, but she forgave him. The impulsive adventure had become involved in a fearsomeness at which she could now smile. The road at any rate led to somewhere. Philip with his dreadful matter of factness, would say that. But Philip wouldn't say anything. There was no Philip. That romance had ended like this one in grim and ugly realism, unmitigated matter of fact.

Richstead New Park was undeniably a cold matter of fact. Ann surveyed it from the edge of the common and wondered what to do next. She might just as well continue to follow her guide. He was pursuing his way along a road of mean and shabby villas. He had not deviated from his straight road. The piper was ploughing his way straight ahead, unmindful of his surroundings, so it seemed. Ann had a kind of feeling that if he met a brick wall he would go through it, playing his pipe the while.

The street of mean villas was the continuation of the road to Nowhere. No, it had been the road to Somewhere. Richstead New Park! The irony of it!

Suddenly it seemed as though they might be heading for a brick wall. The road they were in turned the corner to the right. A building, a garage perhaps, faced them, and some more shabby villas.

No, the building was not a garage, it would be a nonconformist chapel. This kind of neighbourhood always supported dissenting places of worship. The piper headed along at an accelerated pace. Ann felt it was time she began to make enquiries as to her whereabouts. It was no use asking the piper, he was dumb, though friendly. A sight of his smiling old face would be consoling in this very strange and alien place. She would ask at a corner shop. It was precisely the kind of street which would suffer a corner shop gladly. The only house that had not got Nottingham lace curtains and a round table with an "exhibit" on it in the window was one labelled "to let."

Ann suddenly discovered that she was dead beat. The way lay round the corner to the right, or so it seemed to her. But the piper appeared to think otherwise. He seemed bent on following his straight road. When he came to the gate of the chapel-like building, he still kept straight on, through the open gate. He was not piping now, but the spell was still upon her. There was an open door beyond the open gate. She might at least see where the road to Nowhere ended! Her mood was ironical.

Ann stood hesitating on the threshold through which the pied piper had disappeared. Then she pushed the inner door and went in.

The place Ann found herself in was in almost complete darkness. She could discern benches on either side, and a long path between them leading to a bright spot in a shadowy distance. It was a curious cave-like place, with a vaulted roof. In the dim light it was impossible to make out any more. Ann's guide was kneeling in one of the benches. She slipped into another and sat down. How thankful she was to sit down. She found herself gazing along what was, yes, surely—the fantastic idea still held her—the continuation of the road they had followed! It led into the shadows that hung about the far end of the strange building. Her eyes were getting used to the darkness. She could make out an object now, a bright object, shining there, where the "road" ended. The light from a single red lamp which hung above was reflected on it, revealing a burnished golden doorway. Not a doorway that a man's body might pass through, but one which might well give a call to his less mortal parts.

Was it her fancy? Ann sat and wondered. It reminded somehow of the catacombs—this place. What did the little golden doorway mean? What did it all mean? She was tired out and dazed with the sickness of her wounded heart. It was restful here. The old piper had not let her down so badly. He was kneeling in front of her, upright; so rigid and motionless that his spirit might indeed have left his body and gone through the little golden door. What *did* it all mean?

Then a voice fell on her ear. It came from someone hidden from view behind a block of masonry, over where there were candles burning on a stand.

"It has already got its altar-stone," the voice said. "You see, every altar has its consecrated stone, marked with the five wounds of Christ. The wounds in His hands and feet, and the wound in His heart."

Ann listened with all her ears. There was something about the high altar at St. Peter's in Rome! And then something about the martyrs' tombs in the catacombs! But the words that echoed in her ears were those—"The wound in His heart." And they were speaking about a stone?—a wounded stone!

"You see, our church is the church of the catacombs." The speaker and the person he was addressing, suddenly loomed into view. The intruder in the bench just behind them, slipped quickly behind the sheltering pillar. She felt sure she had no business there. She could hear distinctly what was being said.

"We keep the Blessed Sacrament there. People who have received Holy Communion in the morning sometimes like to come back later in the day and say 'thank You'; and others like to find eternity just beyond the little golden door yonder."

Ann could hardly believe her ears. The road to Somewhere went on, through the little golden door in the shadows to Eternity. What an amazing finish to her fantastic dream! She waited eagerly for more.

What *was* that about the stone having wounds on it?

Alack! there came an interruption. Someone had come and summoned the speaker and his companion away. Their footsteps retreated towards the sacristy door. The voice passed out of Ann's hearing. But she sat on, wondering, and not attempting to move. There was the peace, the silence, and above all the marvel of the words she had just heard. The stone of sacrifice marked with the five wounds of Christ. It was a stone marked with five marks which Philip had refused to trample on. When—the thought struck her like a hammer-blow—she, Ann, had bidden him do so.

There were words ringing in her ears, an echo of the tender strain of the pied piper's "vespers."

Chapter Ten

"Deep in His Heart for us
The wound of love He bore;"

The mark in the centre of the stone would be the wound in His heart.

"That love which He enkindles still
In hearts which Him adore."

She glanced at the figure of the old piper. He was still rapt. The heart which adored Him was—saying "thank You" for something? How much more could she learn of this mystery of faith, of this church of the catacombs? But she could not wait to learn any more. She could have stayed on for ever wondering, but there was no time to be lost. Even now Philip might have yielded—he might have surrendered to that last look of hers and given in and paved the pathway to Two Gables with the wounded stone. The stone which bore the holy symbol of the wound which "deep in His heart for us" He, the One who dwelt in an Eternity just beyond the little golden door yonder, had borne for the human beings whom He had drawn to Himself in some strange way that she had yet to understand.

Dear old Philip. He was not romantic, but he was always so true, so right. She felt no need now to misconstrue his "contrariness." She understood. But—what had she done? She must get back to Richstead at once and make sure that it was all right. She had been so uncompromising, and he had looked so terribly pale. He might have given in after she left for he was but human and—he loved her. Why had she ever doubted that he loved her? How could she ever have doubted it?

As for poor Uncle Silas, he was all at sea. There could be no possible connection between the thing he was out against and this, this Somewhere to which the road across the common had led her. Philip was right, as usual. His was a kind of bogey. The two had been completely dissociated in her mind as she sat in the church which was "the church of the catacombs."

It had been exactly like a fairy tale come true.

But Ann was done with dreaming. She fled out of the dream-place into the wide-awake world which housed in yellow brick villas the people who came to say "thank You" for their age-old Mystery of Faith. She must get back to Richstead even if it meant walking across the common in the dark. She knew the way. It was not so far. The round-about way by the road would take too long.

Her heart was no longer heavy like a stone, it was leaping within her. The wound had been miraculously healed. But there remained a wound in Another's heart, and the sign of it was graven on a stone. Oh, what had she done?

The common was very, very lonely, and this time there was no piper to guide and protect her. Ann trudged on, sturdily. Then a sudden panic seized her. Someone was walking behind her. She hastened her pace. The other did the same. She was very nearly crying out when a voice sounded in her ear:

"Ann! Did I frighten you? What on earth are you doing here?"

"Philip! Where have you sprung from?"

Chapter Eleven

THEY STOOD looking at one another.

"You are just the person I wanted," Ann said when she found her breath. She said it in as commonplace a tone as she could command, but it was a pale and panting little Ann. "I was coming back to Two Gables to see about it. Phil, you mustn't put that stone down—James Laydon's stone, I mean. You haven't done it already? You haven't changed your mind?"

He gazed with amazement into the anxious little face. It was anxiety that made her imperious. Whatever miracle had happened?

"Why, Nan," he cried, "*you've* changed your mind. What has happened to you?"

"But you won't change your mind?" She was too eager to make sure to answer his question.

"I can't, Nan. I've got rid of the stone."

Her eyes widened with apprehension. What *had* happened to Nan?

"Got rid of it? Where? How?"

"I have just made a present of it to the padre of the Catholic church down there. I was afraid I might change my mind if I kept it on the premises. But what brought you to Richstead New Park?"

Ann's eyes sparkled. They danced with joy.

"The pied piper. I didn't notice which way I was going and he was in front and he piped me right over the common, and the road went right on into the church, and I followed him. And there happened to be someone in the church talking about altar stones to somebody else. Why, Phil! It must have been you that the priest—I suppose it was the priest—was talking to!"

"It was me, sure enough," Philip said. "It all sounds remarkably queer."

"You mustn't laugh at me, Phil, for it's all ever so real and serious, although the pied piper does come into it."

He certainly didn't look as though he were going to chaff her. "It's extraordinary, Ann. Much more extraordinary than you think. Do you know who it was that popped that book about James Laydon through my letter slot? It came in that way, I discovered. It was the pied piper."

"Phil! You are not joking?"

"No, I'm not, it was quite a simple solution. He overheard us telling Tom about the stone on the Broadway that afternoon, and he happens to be a great man on the Elizabethan Catholics, and knew all about James Laydon, so he thought he would make a present of the book to the inmate of Two Gables."

"I have got to read about James Laydon," Ann said.

"It's very gruesome reading, ladykin."

"Tosh!" she said. "We have got to be real. I hate shams. Richstead New Park is real."

"And James Laydon is gloriously real. He's almost alive."

"I *must* read about him," Ann repeated.

"Talking about realities," Philip said. "Of course, this means good-bye to Two Gables. Uncle Silas won't be likely to go back from his word."

Ann grew grave. "I don't mind a rap about Two Gables," she said. "It is Uncle Silas who is worrying me. He will hate it so. And he has been so good to us. Phil, I hate the idea of his coming round tomorrow and getting that curt answer. If only we could have gone and told him, or written."

Philip pondered. "I can go round to Mincing Lane tomor-row in my lunch hour," he said. "Uncle Silas is always in the office about then."

"And I will come with you," Ann said. "I don't see why you should face it alone. It will be perfectly horrid. Poor Uncle Silas! He will be so furious. He doesn't understand one tiny bit. I *hate* having to hurt him like this."

"And yet—you wouldn't have it otherwise?"

She gave a little shudder. "Phil, I can't think how I could have been so, so horrible! But I didn't know."

She was thinking. "And I don't know what I know now! Only I seem to have had a glimpse through a kind of window and caught sight of a new country stretching away, outside a closed-in place, a great vast upland beyond a little town back-garden."

"The road to Somewhere has led you on to the Never-never Land, Ann?"

"No," she said, thoughtfully. "If it really went on through that little golden gate, it must be the 'for ever and for ever land.'"

He glanced at her sideways. It was glorious to have the old Nan at his side once again. A thin drizzle had begun to fall, but they neither of them noticed it. "Do you remember," he said, "that I told you that you would rather have the moon for a wedding gift than Two Gables?"

"But, Phil, it is not the moon. The moon is all very well, but it doesn't give out a light that never was on sea or land. You think this is all fantastic, like the pied-piper story?"

"Nan, I don't. The pied-piper is not fantastic. He was a true word spoken in jest, if you will. You know," he went on, seri-ously enough, "the padre told me that the old man is a kind of saint and he prays on his pipe. Those Catholics have a quaint way of putting things—especially when they are desperately in earnest."

He had set his companion thinking furiously. The drizzle had turned to a steady rain.

"Don't you think we had better turn back and go home by train from New Park?" Philip said.

"Oh, yes, do let us do that," Ann said, eagerly enough. "I noticed that there was a house to let in the road leading to the church. Arabella Grove, it's called. I like New Park, it's so *real*."

Realism was certainly the outstanding feature of the district known as Richstead New Park. Philip and Ann were fain to admit this as they scoured its precincts in search of the railway station. With no pied piper to guide them they missed Arabella Grove and found themselves ultimately in a road of larger pretensions, which, however, did not rise to a post office where they could ring up Taplow Square and explain that Ann was with her *fiancé* and would not be back to dinner.

"We shall have to ask the way," Philip said. "New Park is pre-eminently a place to get out of."

It certainly was rather an elfish substitute for a land of vision. "I suppose the pied piper lives here," Ann said, facing reality with stubborn approval.

Someone turned round as she made the remark. There followed an exclamation and mutual greetings. The next moment Ann was being introduced to Father Saunders. It was just a little complicated to explain her presence after the confidences of what was scarcely more than half-an-hour ago!

Philip took the bull by the horns. "I found her on the common," he explained. "She had followed the lure of the pied piper; and she has visited your church as well as myself."

"I am delighted to meet Miss Perivale," the padre said. "I should like to hear more of this story in which my friend Carlyon seems to be implicated. Suppose you come in and make use of my telephone; I am afraid you won't get a train back for some time, it is a wretched service, and you might as well wait in comfort." The padre explained to them, in his cheery way, that he had just run out to buy some tobacco. He had a friend with him who was sharing his smoke. "Rolt will be most delighted to meet you," he told Philip. "We have been examining the stone together. I think I told you he has a great devotion to the English martyrs."

The cosy sitting-room in the Presbytery was a welcome change from the streets. "I have one other guest who I think Miss Perivale will be interested to meet," the Father said, with a twinkle in his eye. "I take it that you are not stiff and starched in your social ideas. My other guest is the pied piper. He is not a conversationalist, but he has wide ears, as you know," he smiled across at Philip, "and wide interests. I have this minute dragged him in from the church. He is having supper with us."

The genial padre surveyed the glowing faces before him. "I wonder," he said, impulsively, "if I could persuade you to join us?"

Ann was certain that he could, and said so. Philip admitted himself ready without persuasion. Father Saunders was delighted. Hannah would consider that she was entertaining a pair of angels well awares. She had already been called in to see the relic. The sight of the donor would cure the soreness of her eyes for ever and a day.

It was a truly merry party that sat down to the simple but hospitable repast. Mr. Duncan Rolt was quite the type of the business man, not so unlike Uncle Silas, except that he lacked the platform manner. Ann sat in shy but exquisite enjoyment next to Mr. Carlyon. She felt like one in a dream. Philip was describing Two Gables, and how it had been acquired by his uncle as a bargain.

"It was doubly generous of Mr. Bulkington to be giving it to us," Ann ventured to put in, "when he could have sold it again at a profit."

Mr. Rolt nodded. "I know Mr. Bulkington," he said. "I have had business dealings with him before now. Two Gables would have been a very handsome present. It is a thousand pities that he has those weird prejudices against the Church. And I am afraid he is a man who is not likely to go back on his word."

"I love Uncle Silas," Ann said, "and I hate having to hurt his feelings. I don't mind a fig about Two Gables, but I do mind that."

Father Timothy eyed her approvingly. This was a very gentle Christian little lady. He turned to the silent old man at her side. "You will have to pray for a miracle to be worked on Mr. Bulkington," he said. "Something that will soften the blow, at any rate."

The Christian little lady looked doubtful. "Uncle Silas has got it all wrong," she cried. "The Popery he talks about hasn't got anything in the least to do with—this!"

Duncan Rolt laughed at the naïve remark. "A case of mistaken identity," he suggested.

"Or perhaps one of Mr. Bulkington's ancestors got a bad scare in the reign of Queen Mary and established a hereditary complex. We may, after all, in some way be to blame for 'Bonzo,'" Father Timothy said. "Catholics should not forget that."

Their host insisted on the quaint little festivity ending with a toast. Hannah had produced a bottle of particularly rare (though not in the connoisseur's sense) wine from a cellar mainly given over to other purposes, and she stood over them like a presiding spirit to see that the thing was done properly. If the fatherly relation, in the spiritual sense was suggested by the good padre, material motherliness was embodied in Hannah. She even suggested the maternal smack on occasions. Quite a number of people were frightened of Hannah. She had brought up many a young priest to change his wet boots, and inculcated the penance of flannel next to the skin.

The padre rose from his seat and raised his glass: "To the glorious memory of James Laydon, priest," he said.

Philip obeyed with the others. He set his glass down: "But he isn't a memory," he objected, characteristically. "James Laydon is most tremendously alive."

Chapter Twelve

PHILIP RESTORED Ann to the bosom of her family at quite a reasonably early hour. Fortunately the bosom was meagrely represented by Tom, intent on reconstructing the wireless. He accepted Ann's effusive interest in what he was doing and asked no questions. The others had gone out to Bridge.

Philip and Ann had arranged it all in the train which had condescended to stop at Richstead New Park and pick them up. They would call together on Uncle Silas tomorrow in the lunch hour, and they would do their best to soften the blow. "I can understand how Uncle Silas feels," Ann said, "because I felt like it myself this morning! It seems incredible now that I could have had a 'Bonzo' complex—is that what you call it? It really is an interesting theory—a sort of ancestral scare, instead of something happening just in one's own infancy. But I am afraid we shall never get at Uncle Silas's complex."

It must be admitted that Mr. Bulkington did not look like a promising subject for psycho-analysis when Philip and Ann invaded his lair next day.

Ann glanced fearfully at the grim face behind the impressive desk. Mr. Bulkington had told them to be seated in a most official way. He fixed a cold, enquiring eye on Philip, then, as the latter did not find his words at once, rapped on the table with his knuckles and said, "Well?"

"You have been to Richstead?" Philip stammered, making

a desperate plunge into the matter in hand.

"I have *not*," Mr. Bulkington replied. "I was unable to go round that way this morning. I had an appointment here at an early hour."

Philip's heart sank into his boots. Uncle Silas had been spared the brusque negative answer of the gap in the path, but the whole thing had to be tackled now.

Mr. Bulkington's countenance grew more and more forbidding—grotesquely so—he might almost have been bent on the task of making it forbidding.

"Well?" he repeated, and tapped with his foot on the ground.

Philip blurted it out. "I'm frightfully sorry, Uncle, but I can't bring myself to carry out your condition. It's no good."

The listener's face was exactly like a mask. He turned to Ann. "And you?" he asked. "Are you going to let Two Gables go?"

Ann lifted her eyes to his. Oh, how she hated hurting Uncle Silas!

"I agree with Philip," she said it as gently as she could.

Mr. Bulkington sat regarding her. It was impossible to read exactly what was going on in his mind, but something within him appeared to be causing what are called "conflicting emotions."

"Nonsense," he said, at length. "Ann, I thought you had taken a fancy to the place?"

It was heart-breaking, trying to explain. "I had," she told him. "I had, indeed. But, all the same, I quite agree with Philip." What more could she say?

He turned and addressed his nephew.

"You realize perfectly what you are doing. I am a man of my word. That stone was to have been in its place this morning, and I understand that it is not so? You have not carried out my conditions?"

Philip nodded. "That is so, Uncle."

"You understand the consequence? Two Gables will remain my property to dispose of as I wish. And as for you—I wash my hands of your affairs once for all. You haven't let yourself in for that furniture, have you?"

"No, Uncle," Philip said. "I quite grasped the affair in all its bearings."

Mr. Bulkington continued slowly, "You have realized what this means to Ann?" It was a hard hit. Then he said, very slowly, after a pause: "For Ann's sake I am willing to give you another week to think it over."

But Philip shook his head. "It's settled and done with," he said. "I've given the stone away. I was afraid if I kept it I might change my mind."

He hardly knew what possessed him to drop the bombshell. Ann listened with cold terror in her heart. Uncle Silas might realize that the stone was not Philip's property to give away?

But Uncle Silas was curiously calm. One might almost have said that he was less angry now than before. "Well," he said, "then you have gone and done for yourself. I knew you were mixed up with those Papists. I am not often mistaken. Well, you can't say that I haven't given you a fair chance, can you?"

"Indeed, I can't, Uncle," Philip said, cordially. "I only hope the house won't be on your hands."

Mr. Bulkington smiled—a grim and peculiar smile. "I have just had an offer for it," he said. "You have played the fool to a greater extent than you imagined. But knavery and folly go together," he added, as though by an afterthought. Bonzo was not quite getting his due. "By the way, you are still caretaker of Two Gables. You had better be there this evening. I will ring up this mad American who wants to buy the place and tell him that you will show him over. Any time after 5 o'clock, eh?"

Mr. Bulkington rose and went over to the telephone. "Green's Hotel, Mayfair." He turned and nodded sideways to his visitors, implying that they were dismissed.

Philip and Ann found themselves in the street before either of them spoke. "Well," Philip said at length. "I must say he took it remarkably well."

"Philip"—his *fiancée*'s tone was not devoid of awe—"Do you think the pied piper has been praying on his pipe? Something does seem to have softened the blow. I don't believe Uncle Silas was half as angry as he tried to look."

Philip shook his head. "I am afraid we have got to face life without Uncle Silas as a financial prop. The complex is still there. Two Gables has gone; and my prospects in the Bulkington firm, unless Uncle Silas becomes convinced that he was mistaken in jumping to a conclusion."

"Uncle Silas hates to be mistaken," Ann said, meditatively. She spoke again, after due thought. "There is that house to let in Arabella Grove," she said. "We could manage quite well there. Suppose we go over together this afternoon? I want to say good-bye to Two Gables, and after we have shown the new owner round we could walk over to New Park and have a look at the other house."

"Bravo, Ann!" her lover said.

They snatched a hasty lunch in the tail-end of Philip's lunch hour. Ann insisted on poached eggs as being economical, and that they should devour them in a Lyons tea-shop. "Now," she said, when they had finished. "Whilst you are at the office I will enquire about furnishing on the hire system. They will expect me at home when they see me. They know that we are busy over the furnishing."

The twilight was gathering over Richstead when Philip and Ann found themselves once more on the Broadway. The pied piper had retired from his pitch. It was just as well, Ann said, as she was rather vague about the etiquette with regard to dropping money into the hats of people whom one has dined with. It was a chilly evening and she felt glad that the frail old man was not standing there. She would have loved to be able to bring some comfort into his life. She felt that she stood heavily in the old piper's debt.

Two Gables pricked its rugged ears at the approach of the lovers. "It is a darling old place," Ann said. "It looks quite friendly, and I don't feel a bit like an intruder. I shall always love Two Gables."

"It made you divinely discontented with the Tower House," her companion suggested. Ann meditated.

"And 29 Arabella Grove has made me divinely discontented with Two Gables." They had wandered into the low-roofed dining-room. "And to think," she said, "that since I was here I have had supper with the pied piper. I must tell The Oaks, it will be so shocked."

They sat themselves side by side on the window seat. "Perhaps we shall see James Laydon coming up the path," she said, "instead of the American personage. I hope he won't be late, by-the-bye. I am dying to get on to Arabella Grove. Somebody may have snapped up the house."

"So you still prefer Arabella Grove to this, Nan? You wouldn't change your mind if it were not too late?"

"Phil! Why, it's because we are going to live in Arabella Grove on twopence ha'penny that Two Gables is so glorious. It's real now, not a silly fake. As real as——"

"Digley Grange?" he suggested.

She fell to thinking. "Phil, I want to know more about the road beyond the little golden gate. Do you think Father Saunders would tell me?"

"We will pursue the road to Somewhere and ask him," her sweetheart said, "when we have done with our American. Why, there he is. Wasn't that the gate?"

Ann sprang up. "It's not him," she said. "It's—how curi-ous!—Father Saunders and Mr. Rolt. How lucky they have come now. They would not have been able to get in otherwise."

The next minute Philip had ushered the unexpected visi-tors into the room. "Ann and I are saying Good-bye to Two Ga-bles," he said, cheerfully, "but we think we have found a place to suit us, over in your part. My Uncle has found a purchaser for this place. I'm just expecting him to have a look over it."

Father Saunders was smiling. "Let me introduce you to him," he said. "Mr. Rolt has just purchased Two Gables, and he has a proposition to make."

Philip gazed at the businesslike looking man at the priest's side. Mr. Rolt smiled. "I saw Mr. Bulkington this morning, early," he said. "I made him an offer for Two Gables, but he told me someone else had the refusal. I tried to tempt him, but it was no good. I offered him"—the speaker named a sum that took the listener's breath away—"but he couldn't be bribed; not until he had heard the other's decision. He closed with me at my terms later on."

"But," Philip gasped. "Didn't you realize that it was me whom he was alluding to? You need only have waited and you could have got the place for a sixth of what you have given."

"Possibly," Duncan Rolt said. "But then I should not have had the satisfaction of finding out exactly what lengths Silas Bulkington was prepared to go to before he broke his word. A man with the disgusting amount of money I have, doesn't often get a chance of purchasing a novel satisfaction. A business deal is the breath of Mr. Bulkington's nostrils. He has played the game magnificently with you and your bride-elect. Your uncle may have quaint ideas about popery but he understands cricket."

Ann broke in: "And he gave us another week to think it over. Uncle Silas has been a brick. I did so hate having to hurt him. But," she added, "perhaps this has softened the blow a little."

Duncan Rolt smiled at the eager face. Yes, his money had been well spent in softening the blow.

"Suppose we ring him up and see," he said.

He stepped over to the telephone.

The next minute they were listening to the one-sided conversation.

"Mr. Bulkington? Ah, yes, I'm delighted with Two Gables. Glad to secure it at the figure I mentioned. Your nephew has shown me everything. I hope he may continue to act as caretaker for me. I propose to furnish the place but I shall not be living in it, so I shall need a caretaker. It might suit your nephew and his wife when he marries——"

The speaker paused and listened to the reply. He smiled. The arrangement had evidently been satisfactory.

"Well, good-bye," he said, and hung up the receiver.

A wide-eyed Ann was standing listening.

"What did Uncle Silas say?" she asked.

"He said: 'I'm very glad, very glad indeed. Poor little Ann fancied the place.'"

"Good old Uncle Silas!" Philip said. He looked as though he wanted to add: "Good old somebody else!" but didn't quite like to.

"You heard what I said about asking you to be caretaker?" Duncan Rolt said. "I should ask you to see to the furnishing as well. I shall not be living at Two Gables myself, but possibly, later on I might ask a favour of you. I would like Mr. Carlyon to end his days in comfort in Two Gables. Would you have any objection to a paying guest?"

Ann clapped her hands. "Oh, indeed I would," she cried. "But I would love to take in a lodger."

Father Saunders was looking intently at the glowing face.

"Miss Ann," he said. "I believe we met once before, many years ago. Do you remember a certain wishing well where everybody was told to wish for something?"

"Why, of course I do," she cried. "I wished, ever so hard, that the once-upon-a-time-things might be true."

"And I prayed that you might find them so," he said.

Ann looked at the grave face of the speaker, he was regarding her with a kindly penetration in his gaze.

"I remember you," she said, slowly. "You must be the clergyman who laughed when everybody else was serious, and who was serious—Oh, how I *loved* you for it!—when everybody else laughed."

"Very well described," Duncan Rolt said. "I was there myself. I remember Father Tim would have it that it was a holy well."

Father Tim was still meditating on the subject of the Ann behind the glowing little face with the big, shining brown eyes. He consulted his watch. "I have to be back to Benediction," he observed. "I always have a short, quite simple Benediction at 6.30 on Tuesdays." He turned to Ann. "You have never been to Benediction, of course?"

"I don't even know what it is," she confessed.

"Well," he suggested, "if we all walked over the common together, along your 'road to Somewhere' you would be able to find out. At Benediction I open the golden gate."

.   .   .   .   .

For the second time Ann found herself kneeling in the church that suggested the catacombs. On this occasion some slight attempt had been made at lighting, and on the altar half-a-dozen small candles were burning. A fair number of people, all of them poor folk, were dotted about the benches.

The priest in his cotta and stole knelt before the altar, and on the altar the little golden gate stood wide open! Heads had been lowered as it opened to the sweet strains of a tune familiar to Ann.

The children were singing a hymn: "Sweet Sacrament divine." Ann recognized the tune. The pied piper had played it out on the common yesterday. Could it be only yesterday? Such great things had happened since yesterday. Such story-booky things! Yet the greatest of all lay here in waiting.

What did it all mean?

It was all so wonderful. The enchanted road had led her back into the work-a-day. She had glimpsed reality. Arabella Grove had triumphed over Two Gables—the Two Gables of leisured Suburbia, not the Two Gables of James Laydon and Cecil Carlyon, and it might be other inmates of his ilk. (They had talked of this, walking over the common, she and Duncan Rolt.) How glorious it was that the road to Never-never Land had led her to New Park.

There was a hush in the singing. The priest was wearing something over his shoulders. He stepped forward, knelt down, rose again, and stretched out his hands into the Infinity beyond the golden gate.

The heads in front were bowed down. Philip was kneeling at her side and his head was lowered, too. He would be saluting the Faith of his friend, James Laydon.

Now the priest was facing them. There was something in his hands, but it was hidden beneath a silken veil. She must wait to learn more about "the mystery of faith," once delivered to the saints in a Once which was also Now.

She bowed her head with the others. This much she knew, that the stone of Sacrifice paved the way to the Gate, not to be trampled on and scorned, but as a symbol of the real road, the great, gallant way, with crosses strewn upon it. She was still outside. But Benediction had indeed opened the golden gate, and beyond there stretched, onward and onward, the Road to Somewhere.

The priest had gone from the altar and the lights had been extinguished, but Ann knelt on, until she felt a touch on her arm.

"Sorry, darling," said Philip's voice, "but I think we ought to try for the 7.40 to Waterloo."

ALSO BY ENID DINNIS

View a sample chapter from each title at www.staidanpress.com.

THE ANCHORHOLD

Editha de Beauville had all that the world could offer: wealth, wit, and beauty. Yet a chaplain's sermon drove her to give up all this, and enter the religious life. But could a proud, strong-willed noblewoman accept and embrace the poverty and self-abnegation of the religious life, particularly that of full seclusion in an anchorhold? A difficult path lay before Editha. Read on to learn how she fared, and how her life affected those around her, including Sir Aleric, her erstwhile suitor, now a crusader knight; Fr. Nicholas, a young priest who was quite bright, and thought so too; and Fiddlemee, the witty yet wise court jester whose past held a surprising secret.

$14.00 — 194 pages. Available at amazon.com.

THE SHEPHERD OF WEEPINGWOLD

Sir Robert Luffkyn, rich grandson of a peasant, has purchased the manor of Weepingwold from the noble but impoverished de Lessels, intending to make the renamed Luffkynwold a busy center of his tanning trade. He sends Petronilla, last de Lessels, to Gracerood, intending her for its future Abbess, and plucks little Brother Kit from the cloister to become the new parson of the long-abandoned church. How will Father Kit fare with the parish and his own soul? What is Petronilla's true vocation? And is there really a witch in the parish?

$14.00 — 202 pages. Available at amazon.com.

OTHER TITLES AVAILABLE FROM ST. AIDAN PRESS

THE QUEEN'S TRAGEDY
by Msgr. Robert Hugh Benson

"Upon the publication of former books of mine several kindly critics remarked that the reign of Mary Tudor told a very different story with regard to the Catholic character. It is that story which I am now attempting to set forth as honestly as I can."

$19.00 — 364 pages. Available at amazon.com.

THE NET
by Agnes Blundell

"Roger felt a freezing dew break out upon his forehead. The net was over him it seemed; in vain he told himself that he could establish his identity. His head was worth forty pounds to the vile creatures at the stair foot, and once in their clutches who knew if he could ever communicate with his friends? . . . Gaolers and pursuivants alike fattened on the traffic in human life and divided the spoils. Judges were as careless as callous."

$16.00 — 264 pages. Available at amazon.com.

REDROBES
by Fr. Neil Boyton

Thirteen-year-old orphan Jacques gets into trouble in Quebec, and decides to run away to Huronia and become an interpreter for his Jesuit guardian, Father John Brebeuf. But his journey along the Iroquois-infested river may not be so easy as he hopes!

$17.00 — 300 pages. Available at amazon.com.

SCOUTING FOR SECRET SERVICE
by Fr. Bernard F. J. Dooley

Frank and George are going to spend their summer vacation in the Adirondacks, thanks to Frank's uncle Ed. But once they get there, they realize something fishy is going on. Can they trust Pete, their Indian guide, or is he mixed up in it too? And is Frank's mysterious uncle really behind it all?

$14.00 — 188 pages. Available at amazon.com.

THE MASTERFUL MONK
by Fr. Owen Francis Dudley

Brother Anselm comes back to England to counter the Atheist's efforts to destroy the influence of Catholic morals. Between his lectures he is drawn into a struggle for the soul of Beauty Dethier, who is Catholic but fascinated by the "freedom" of the world and the Atheist. It will take more than argument to save her from disaster.

$18.00 — 342 pages. Available at amazon.com.

WILL MEN BE LIKE GODS? AND THE SHADOW ON THE EARTH
by Fr. Owen Francis Dudley

Father Dudley's first two books on human happiness are published together here—his rare collection of essays together with a novel which illustrates the essays and introduces his most famous character, the Masterful Monk.

$15.00 — 216 pages. Available at amazon.com

CANDLELIGHT ATTIC AND ODD JOB'S
by Cecily Hallack

"I am continually hearing stories—exquisite ones—which would be proof enough to any soul that God is an Infinitely Understanding Person. But usually for the very reason of their nature, they are private—keepsakes between the soul and God."

$14.00 — 192 pages. Available at amazon.com.

THE HAPPINESS OF FATHER HAPPÉ
by Cecily Hallack

Shingle Bay did not know what to make of Fr. Savinius Happé. He was a cheerful, rotund Franciscan, a famous author of books on everything from Etruscan civilization to Alpine meadows to beetles, and someone who had never quite mastered the English language. His jovial demeanor concealed a wisdom that alternately bewildered, astonished, but ultimately won over the people of Shingle Bay.

$10.00 — 112 pages. Available at amazon.com.

THE RED INN OF SAINT LYPHAR
by Anna T. Sadlier

Once Saint Lyphar was a happy village in France, ruled by a generous Marquis and taught by the good Curé. Now the Révolution has put the Curé to death, and the villagers are about to rise under the famous leader Jambe d'Argent. But a Revolutionary spy is lurking near the Inn. . . .

$13.00 — 168 pages. Available at amazon.com.

CON OF MISTY MOUNTAIN
by Mary T. Waggaman

"It had been a long night for Con. Just what had happened to him he was at first too dazed to know. Dennis had flung him into the smoking-room with no very gentle hand, turned the key and left him to himself. And, sinking down dully upon a rug that felt very soft and warm after the hard flight over the mountain, Con was glad to rest his bruised, aching limbs, his dizzy head, without any thought of what was to come upon him next."

$14.00 — 190 pages. Available at amazon.com.

NON-FICTION

THE STORY OF THE WAR IN LA VENDÉE AND THE LITTLE CHOUANNERIE
by George J. Hill, M. A.

The story of the brave French Catholics who rose up in arms against the revolutionary government.

$18.00 — 342 pages. Available at amazon.com.

CATHOLICISM AND SCOTLAND
by Compton Mackenzie

The little known history of the Scots who sought to defend their country and their Faith from the onslaught of Protestantism.

$12.00 — 138 pages. Available at amazon.com.

DOMINICAN SAINTS
by the Novices of the Dominican House of Studies

The astonishing lives of fourteen saints of the Dominican Order, with an encyclical on the Dominican Order by Pope Benedict XV and a list of all the Dominican Saints and Blesseds (as of 1921).

$19.00 — 392 pages. Available at amazon.com.